Broken Glass

His Warriors

Book 1

By

Ronna M. Bacon

Psalms 51:17. The sacrifices of God are a broken spirit; a broken and a contrite heart, O God, You will not despise.

Isaiah 57:15. For thus says the high and exalted One Who lives forever, whose name is Holy, "I dwell on a high and holy place, and also with the contrite and lowly of spirit in order to revive the spirit of the lowly and to revive the heart of the contrite.

(Scripture from the New King James Version)

Table of Contents

Cold rain pelted the three mourners standing near the three coffins. The man held the hands of the young boy and girl, who were not more than ten. He had no words to explain to them why the girl's parents and the boy's mother had been killed in that accident, nor why they would never be coming home again.

The man looked up as the minister stopped to speak with them, nodding at something that was said. He finally turned the children to walk away, the girl looking back, tears mingling with the rain on her face.

The man searched the area. He could feel something off but had no idea of what it was. Why did he feel like someone was watching them?

The dark-garbed figure drew back even further into the darkness of the storm. He chuckled in glee, knowing he was safe at last. He would watch and see if anything came up, but he was sure he had taken care of all the loose ends. His eyes turned once more to the man and the two children, and he cackled in glee once more. He had no remorse in his body. It was just an accident after all, wasn't it?

The man tucked the children into his vehicle, then stood, the rain dripping off his face and clothing as he stared around, uncomfortable. He finally shrugged and slid into the car, putting it in drive and leaving, his heart breaking at the sobs of the girl and the silent tears of the boy. They were his now to raise, he thought. Lord, You'll have to help me. What do I know about raising children?

Chapter 1

Settling his hat back on his head of dirty blond hair that scraped along his jacket collar, Josiah Silverthorn stared through the windshield as the nondescript shop in front of him. Why he was here, he still wasn't sure, but when a friend asked him to check on his cousin and his uncle, he couldn't say no. He planned to be on his way again this afternoon. Surely, it wouldn't take that long to stop in and pass on Noah's greetings to them. Sighing, he slid from the seat and slowly shut the door of his beat-up old pickup truck. He was tired and wanting to find that small town he could hide in, away from all the troubles that had followed him for so many years.

"Go into web designing. It's a nice safe occupation," they said. Josiah snorted. Right, he thought, a nice safe job that had palled and left no challenge for him.

His head shot up as he heard the sound of breaking glass and he strode towards the shop door, his boot heels stirring up dust as he walked forward. He listened for a moment, then cautiously opened the door.

Loud voices greeted him as well as the sound of more breaking glass. This can't be good, he thought. He made his way as silently as he could towards the back of the shop, noting in passing the beautiful stained glasswork displayed. Who was the artist, he wondered?

He paused, his dark brown eyes scanning the area and then focusing on the young woman facing the heavyset man standing in front of her, defiant in her stance. His eyes searched further and saw the older man on the floor, his back against a wall, blood dripping from a wound on his head. His eyes traced back to the young woman as she reached for the glass the man was holding. A sweep of his arm and she went tumbling to the cement floor, a cry of pain wrenched from her before she lay still.

The man stood over her, speaking, his words not audible to Josiah. Josiah moved towards them, unable to stop him from throwing the glass he held towards the wall, where it shattered, flowing to the floor in broken splinters of colour.

As the man turned to gather more glass, Josiah reached for his arm, pulling it behind him. The man struggled, his weight throwing Josiah off balance. With a shove, the man sent Josiah to the floor, where a kick to the ribs sent dark shards of pain through his body.

Josiah shook his head, cautiously sitting upright. The man had gone, a trail of destruction in the work room left behind him. Movement from the older man had Josiah rising and making his way towards him, helping him to his feet.

"Are you okay?"

The man nodded, his hand swiping at the blood on his face. "He's gone?" When Josiah nodded, the man stared around at the destruction. "There was no need for this. Why?" Then his eyes lit on the young woman crumpled on the floor. "Faith! Faith!" He dropped to his knees, hand reaching to touch her auburn hair.

Josiah dropped down on the other side of her. He had taken rudimentary first aid but knew her injury was likely beyond what help he could administer.

"Call 911." Josiah looked up at the man. "Please, call."

The man hesitated, not wanting to leave, and Josiah, with a mutter of dismay, handed him his phone.

"Can you call 911?" Josiah held the phone out once more, until it was taken. Then his attention turned to the young woman.

Green eyes filled with tears of pain and fear opened and searched for the older man. He could see a quick flicker of relief spread through them.

"Where are you hurt?" His quiet voice caught her attention.

"My shoulder and my back." She tried to move, and the pain stopped her, bringing more tears to her eyes. "I can't be laid up. I have too much to do."

Josiah's hand on her arm turned her face back to him. "We've got an ambulance coming." He looked around. "What was that all about?"

Her eyes watched him, then turned past him as the older man returned.

"Faith, Child. Where did he hurt you?"

"My shoulder again, Uncle Seth." Tears of frustration and pain appeared on her face. "Doc warned me if I hurt it again, that meant surgery." She tried to rise and fell back. "Why did he have to come around? We've been through this before."

"Hush, Child. We'll figure it out. Here's Ezra and Deb."

Seth Lockwood moved back to stand near Josiah, his eyes on his niece, hands clenched in anger. The two men listened to the quiet conversation and watched as Faith was lifted to the stretcher and then the stretcher wheeled out.

Seth sighed, turning to look at the broken glass strewn throughout the workroom, his left hand going to rest on the top of his head. "How, Lord, are we to meet our deadlines with this mess and Faith laid up? How, Lord? Why this, Lord?"

Josiah listened, not sure anymore that Someone who couldn't be seen really cared what was happening there.

"What can I do to help?" Josiah's voice startled Seth who spun to stare at him.

"You're still here?" At Josiah's nod, Seth turned once more to look at the shop. "I need to get to the hospital with Faith, but I can't leave this." He reached for a broom.

Josiah's hand stopped him and Seth looked up at him.

"I'm a friend of Noah's. He wanted me to stop in to see how you two were. My name's Josiah Silverthorn. Let me either help you clean up or do the clean up for you."

Seth stopped once again, his eyes taking on a faraway look. "Noah. He needs to come home. We miss him." He looked back at Josiah. "If you're a friend of Noah's, I trust you. Here's the key to the shop. And here's the password for the security system. Let me show you how it works." He pointed at the work table. "There're gloves there. Use them."

Two hours later, Josiah straightened up. The shop floor was clean once more. He had sorted the glass as he picked it up, saving the larger pieces into boxes in the hopes that they could be re-used.

He turned, his thoughts returning to the officer that had responded. He snorted. Nothing's going to get done, he thought. That man shouldn't be wearing a badge; he had no interest in the assault or damage done.

Locking the door behind him, Josiah stood for a moment, eyes searching the area around him. He felt the eyes, the sense of danger. Who was it? He wasn't a praying man, his faith long since deserted. He had had no need for it during the last fifteen years and didn't think he ever would again. God hadn't been there when he really needed him. Sighing, he reached for his keys, stopping as his eyes lit on an object in the pathway. Reaching for it, he fingered it, not quite sure what it was. He shrugged, shoving it into his jeans' pocket as he walked for his truck.

Seth turned as he heard boots hitting the floor behind him and reached to shake

Josiah's hand and accept the keys offered him.

"Did you get it all cleaned up already?"

Josiah nodded. "I did. I saved as much as I could, just in case you can use it. Overall, there wasn't that much I had to throw away. But that's no consolation if you're needing the larger pieces for your work." His eyes strayed towards the door of the waiting room and a frown appeared. What was the man from today doing there? He excused himself and started towards him, causing the man to turn and walk rapidly away. Josiah turned back, finding Seth with a troubled frown on his face.

"Seth?" Josiah's quiet question broke his concentration. "What's this all about?"

Seth shook his head. "Not your concern, young fellow." He sighed. "At least, I didn't think it was. With Noah sending you to see how we are, that sort of changes things." He looked past Josiah. "Ted, what news do you have?"

Dr. Ted Watson approached Seth, his eyes glancing at and dismissing Josiah.

"She's lucky, Seth. Nothing broken but she did manage to dislocate her shoulder again. She'll not be working for a few weeks and then will have to have physiotherapy."

Seth waved his hands in the air. "Never mind that now. Can I see her?"

"For a few minutes." The physician stepped back as Seth moved towards him, pulled Josiah with him. "Only you, Seth."

"Oh, shut up, Ted. It's time you learned that just because you're a doctor that doesn't give you the right to order people around. Faith and I have had this out with you before. This young man's going with me. God has spoken to me about him."

Ted held up his hands but not before Josiah caught the dark look of hatred and dislike thrown at him. Now, what's that about? Josiah wondered, then shrugged. That man's attitude wasn't his problem.

Chapter 2

$\mathcal{S}$eth turned as the door to the shop opened. A smile lit his face as he saw who entered.

"Can't stay away?"

Josiah shot a quick glance at him. "No, I couldn't.   This shop has me fascinated. But first, how's Faith?" Josiah had stayed for a while with Seth last night, watching as the older man had sat beside her bed as she moved restlessly in a pain-filled sleep.

"She's wants out of the hospital now. I said I'd pick her up in about an hour, but I have to work on orders. And I know she's going to want to come here instead of home to rest." Seth was troubled, torn between what he wanted to do and what he had to do. His eyes raised to the ceiling as he communed with the Lord, then he nodded. His eyes lit on Josiah. "You! You're here at

16

just the right time. You can go pick up Faith and bring her home."

Josiah's hand rose. "Hey, I'm just a stranger to you both. You don't know me well enough."

Seth shook his head, turning as the door opened again. He gave a soft groan and Josiah heard him muttering under his breath, not quite catching what he said.

The officer from the day before, Brownlee, Josiah thought his name was, stood before Seth.

"No luck on any of the evidence, Seth. No fingerprints to match."

Seth stared at him, then shook his head. "That's what you say no matter whose business has been damaged. Just go, will you?"

Brownlee stared at Seth. "Don't go making waves, Seth. You remember what happened to Jonathan."

Seth spun to face him, shaking a finger at him. "I remember that he came to the police and no one helped him out. Just get out of here, all right?"

Josiah waited until the door closed, then walked over to watch out the window.

"What's going on here, Seth?" He turned as silence greeted his words.

Seth stood, head and shoulders bowed, before he raised his head once more, an unreadable look on his face. "I don't rightly now any more, Josiah. Someone's moving into our town and trying to take it over."

"And they want you to pay protection money, is that it?"

Seth nodded, a sad look on his face. "If we don't, what you saw yesterday is what we face. It's coming to the point we're ready to pack up and move on, only we don't know where to move to."

"And you're worried about your niece? She was standing up for you both yesterday, but she's not strong enough to fight back in a physical manner."

"That's right. This shouldn't be happening." Seth turned to face the work table, pulling the order book over to him. "If we don't get our orders out this week, we'll be too far behind to catch up. And

Faith just isn't going to be able to." He stopped, as a thought crossed his mind.

"You're thinking that was the whole point of yesterday?"

Seth nodded, not turning, sadness, anger, despair tinging his voice. "I'm afraid it was, Josiah. She has a talent with the stained glass that very few have. She designs the pattern, then makes it. I can do the soldering, but she is the one who cuts the glass. Now, I don't know what we're going to do."

"Let me go and get Faith. We'll come back here and make plans." Josiah watched at Seth turned to him. "I'm at loose ends right now. I'm pretty precise with what I do. Let me see if I can help you cut the glass. Do you have enough of what you need?"

Seth shrugged. "Until Faith can review our supplies, I won't know. If we don't, we'll not get an order back to us in time."

"Where do your supplies come from?"

"Logan City. It's not that far, but we would need a truck to pick it up."

Josiah grinned at him. "I just happen to have one and it's at your disposal. I'll be back."

Anxious to get back to the shop, Faith paced the hospital room. Uncle Seth should have been here by now, she thought. Then, she stopped, heart in mouth at the thought that something had happened to him. Lord, keep him safe. Help us to accomplish what we need to so we can fulfill our orders. How, I'm not sure, Lord, now that I'm handicapped for a few weeks. She sighed, turning as the door was pushed open and her nurse appeared with a wheelchair.

"Here we go, Faith. Your ride's here."

Faith's eyes stared at her, then past her at the tall younger man standing in the doorway, his hat held in his hands. He seemed familiar, but she wasn't sure of who he was.

Josiah watched the conflicting emotions crossing Faith's face and sighed. This was not going how he wanted it to. Thanks, Seth. He approached her and stopped as she backed away, the nurse an interested onlooker.

"Good morning, Faith. Your uncle asked me to pick you up this morning. He's sorting through the orders. He also told me that Noah needed to come home." A smile broke out on Josiah's face. "I'm Josiah, a good friend of your cousin."

Faith caught the look of warning in his eyes and just kept herself from nodding. Interesting, Lord. Who has Noah sent for us to rehabilitate now?

"Thank you, Josiah. It's nice of you to come. Noah's mentioned you many times, always promising to bring you to visit. Now he's sent you on ahead. Glad you finally took his advice and headed our way." She turned to walk to the door, and her nurse was in front of her.

"Wheelchair, my dear."

Faith looked down at it, then up at Josiah. He caught her faint nod and approached, his arm crooked so she could take it.

"Hospital policy or not, I don't think Faith will be needing the wheelchair." The nurse stood, mouth open, as the two walked away, Faith's head at the level of Josiah's shoulder.

Waiting for the elevator, Josiah felt eyes on him, and turning in such a manner that it didn't seem obvious, looked around. The physician from the night before was standing outside the room Faith had been in, a dark angry look on his face.

Faith stood, staring at the truck seat, trying to determine the best way she could get up on it. Josiah stood behind her, watching, waiting for her to ask for help. Then he sighed. Nope, he thought, there is no way she'll ask for help, and we need to get her out of here. He gathered her up into his arms and set her on the seat, a small yelp escaping from her, and reached to fasten her seatbelt. She turned startled eyes on him.

"Sorry. I thought you needed some help." A faint grin creased his face, his teeth showing white again the neatly trimmed, reddish-tinted beard he wore.

"I did, but I wish you had warned me." She stared at him, wondering once again who he was and why Noah had sent him to them.

Climbing behind the wheel, Josiah reached to turn the key in the ignition, then stopped. He needed to talk to Faith about yesterday but wasn't quite sure how.

"Josiah?"

He heard the question in her voice. "Yes, Faith?"

"You're in deep thought. Talk to me about what you found yesterday after you two sent me away." He heard the resignation in her voice.

"I was able to salvage a number of larger pieces of glass. Your uncle says he doesn't know if you'll have enough to finish the work, or if you'll even be able to finish it."

Faith leaned her head back on the headrest as Josiah pulled away from the hospital, his eyes watching as a car followed him. "That's the problem, Josiah. We have a number of orders that shouldn't be a problem to finish, but I'm not able to do the cutting now. And that's the main part of it. The cutting is so precise. Uncle Seth can't do it any more; the arthritis in his one hand makes it too painful."

Josiah watched as the car pulled past them, then spoke, "How be I try my hand at it?   I have never cut stained glass, but I enjoy wood carving and that's pretty precise."

She nodded, the pain in her shoulder sharp at times. "We'll see." She stared out the window. "Who responded?"

"Who responded? Oh, you mean, the police? Someone named Brownlee, I think it was."

She snorted, causing him to stare at her. "He's useless. He's in someone's back pocket. I just wish I knew who. Then maybe we could stop this nonsense."

"I got the impression he wasn't really trying too hard." He pulled to a stop in front of the shop, then reached to place a hand on her arm. "Wait. I'll come around and help you out. Just so you know, I have nowhere I really need to be.   I can work from anywhere. Please let me help you."

Her eyes studied him, reservation deep in them. She knew they needed help, but what could one man do and a stranger at that? Lord, is this one of those times You say just to trust you? It sure feels like it.

Josiah followed her through the shop to the workroom, wondering why he had offered to help. He wasn't even sure that this was where he wanted to be. But it wasn't inherent in him to walk away from someone in need, especially someone as beautiful as Faith.

Seth looked up from his paperwork, then approached his niece, giving her a careful hug.

"How are you feeling?" He started to laugh at the look on her face. "About like that, is it? Sit, my dear. I've got some food here for you. Josiah, I don't suppose you've eaten?"

Josiah shook his head. "It's okay. I'm good."

Seth shook his head and pointed to a stool. "Sit. You've offered to help. We need to make plans." He set sandwiches in front of them, then set mugs down, the aroma of freshly brewed coffee rising from them.

Faith pushed her plate away and cupped her left arm with her hand. She watched her uncle, seeing how deep in thought he was.

"Where do we stand, Uncle Seth?"

He shook his head, a sadness crossing his face. "It looks as if we'll have to restock the glass. Even if we have it today, we'd be working long hard hours to get caught up, and you just can't do it."

Faith nodded. "It's what I figured. We're done then, are we? We'll just pack up and move on, find something else to do, and pray this doesn't happen again." Defeat rested on her face and in her words.

Josiah listened to them, his eyes scanning the area, finally rising and heading for the scrap glass. He fished out a piece and looked for the glass cutter, returning to hand them to Faith.

"Draw me a line on that, Faith, straight, crooked, curved."

She stared at him, then down at the piece of glass as he repeated himself. She shared a look with her uncle, who shrugged. Finally, she reached for the China marker and drew a straight line, shoving the piece of glass back at Josiah. He grinned at the look on her face, then reached for the gloves. Carefully, he traced the line she had drawn, trying to get the right amount of pressure without breaking the glass.

"Now, tell me. Will this break?"

She reached for it, inspected it and then sat watching him. "You've never done this before?"

He shook his head. "No, I haven't, not stained glass. My father was a glazier and I used to help him cut the glass he needed."

Faith and Seth share a glance. Just maybe, Seth thought, we can do this.

"Okay. Let's try a different kind of line. Find me another piece of glass." Faith drew numerous lines, with Josiah tracing them, gaining more confidence with each one.

Faith finally sat back. "Are you sure you don't have to be somewhere?"

He shook his head. "I'm self employed, a website designer, and can work from anywhere. I don't have set hours. Right now, I've put some designs on the back burner. I needed some time."

Faith studied him once more. "Then I want to hire you. We have a website that isn't really what we want. I also have the feeling that someone's been hacking into it. Things aren't they same as they were when I set it up." She stood and paced the work room, finally standing in front of their supply of glass. "Uncle Seth, we'll need to place that order, only I don't know how we'll get it here this week. Their delivery day is past."

Seth walked over and hugged his niece. "Josiah has offered to get it for us. You can order it, then go with him to pick it up. It takes them a while to get it ready. While you're waiting you can help me lay out some of those designs you were working on. If we have to, we'll use some of the display models to fill the orders." He bowed his head and Josiah could hear soft words.

Chapter 3

Faith stared at the man behind the counter. "What do you mean, our order isn't ready? I spoke to Will himself two hours ago and he assured me it would be."

The clerk shrugged. "It's not and won't be until next week."

Faith turned to stare at Josiah, a devastated look on her face. Josiah walked forward.

"The owner of this company, that would be William Alton?"

The clerk stared Josiah up and down and then slowly nodded.

"That's what I thought." Josiah reached for his wallet and pulled out a business card. "Take this to him now and tell him I want to speak with him."

"Not happening."

"I say it is. His office down the hall there?" Josiah was gone before the man could stop him.

Faith could hear a surprised voice raised in happy greeting and then low murmurs. She turned away from the smirk on the clerk's face.

Hearing footsteps behind her shortly, she turned to find Josiah and Will walking towards her. Will stopped at his clerk's side.

"You're through, Pete. This is not the first time you've tried this trick with our good customers. Here's a cheque for the rest of the week's pay. Don there behind you will go with you, so you can gather your things. Hand over your keys. And don't think this will be the end of it. I would suggest you move towns."

Faith stood and stared, her eyes bouncing between the men, waiting until Will finally turned to her.

"I had your order already for you, Faith, and someone decided to dump it. That's why it's not ready. I just found out about it when Josiah here came looking for me. Give me ten minutes and you'll be on your way. No charge for this order." At

Faith's protest, he held up his hands. "No, you deserve to have a free order. It shouldn't have happened."

Faith studied the man driving the truck, wondering again why he was there. Why, Lord? Why him and now? What is it about him that makes me want to trust him? I haven't found that in many men in this town. There's a corruption that runs deep, and I just don't know if I have it in me to fight it any more. Lord, please guide, protect us. Provide that strong tower we need.

"All set? Do you need to stop anywhere else now that we're on the way?" Josiah watched as she thought it through, her lower lip caught between her teeth.

"No, I think we're good. Uncle Seth didn't say if we needed anything else." She turned to look in the box of the truck, where Josiah had strapped down the cartons containing the glass and the lead cames that she had picked out as well.

"All right, then. We're set to go."

Thirty minutes later, Josiah groaned, then signalled to pull off to the side of the road. Faith glanced at him, then at the red and blue lights flickering in the mirror.

"Josiah?"

"Just sit tight. We've done nothing and the police from your town don't patrol out here." He reached for his wallet, pulling out his driver's license and the folder containing his ownership and insurance, rolling down the window when he was finished.

The officer stopped, hand stilling as he reached for the documents Josiah had in his hand. He looked through the window at Faith, then back at Josiah.

"It's okay, Josiah. I don't need those."

Josiah's head spun around, and then he reached to put his documents away. Bill Waters stood there, a friend from the town he had just left.

"What's going on, Bill?"

"Someone phoned in a complaint about a truck with a loose load. It was your plate number. When I ran the plate, I didn't really think it would be you, but we had to check it out." Bill looked into the truck bed.

"Still cautious, I see?" a grin piercing the grim look on his face.

Josiah stared through the window. "I am. Where did the call originate, if you can tell me?"

"That's the strange thing, Josiah. It came from Noah's town."

"About what I figured. This is Noah's cousin, Faith. She had an incident yesterday, assaulted and damage done to her stained glass studio." He turned to Faith. "I'll be right back."

She gave a hesitant nod, then watched as Josiah and Bill stood near the front of the truck, speaking.

"What did you get yourself into, Josiah?" Bill's eyes studied his friend, seeing the stress and strain still there. They had all been worried about him, constantly keeping him in prayer.

"I don't rightly know. Noah asked me to drop in on his uncle and cousin, and I walked in on an assault in progress. The police officer who responded is a joke. Claims there's no evidence, but the man wasn't wearing gloves." Josiah's voice slowed as he thought it through. "That doesn't make a lot of sense, now does it?"

"No, it doesn't. Did you get his name?"

"Brownlee." Josiah turned to Bill at the silence that followed. "You know something about him?"

"I do, and nothing good." He tipped his head towards the truck where Faith sat. "Watch her. If he's acting like that, then something's up."

"I will. I'm going to be trying to help them meet their order goal this week, but they're not sure they'll be able to."

"Stained glass, isn't it? Noah says his uncle does the leading and that Faith designs and cuts. They'll need someone to do the cutting."

"I've offered. I used to cut window panes for Dad, but it's not the same." Josiah thought for a moment. "I wish I knew someone who could help."

Bill grinned at him. "I do, and I'll send her your way tomorrow."

"Bill? Who?"

"My Mom. She does some stained glass art and sells it in Adriel's store in Riverville."

The two men shook hands and Josiah set off once more, eyes watching. Bill followed him until he had to turn back.

"What was that all about, Josiah?"

"Someone was trying to stop us." He searched the surrounding area. "Your trouble's not over, Faith, not by a long shot. On the other hand, Bill's mother's a stained glass artist, and he's sending her our way tomorrow."

Faith stared at him. "Tomorrow?"

Josiah sighed, knowing he had stepped in where he shouldn't have. "I'm sorry, Faith. I should have asked." He pulled over to the side of the road once more, pulling out his phone.

"No, it's okay, Josiah. I'm not so proud that I'll turn down help, not with me handicapped."

"Are you sure?"

She nodded, then looked behind her. "Once we get this inside the shop, then we can decide what we need to do. I know

Uncle Seth will have been working on it already."

Josiah turned from placing the last box, turned and saw Seth and Faith in an attitude that he figured meant they were praying, and walked from the shop back outside. Something was off out there, and he wanted to check it out. Now, what was it he had seen?

Chapter 4

Faith came looking for Josiah later, stopping as she watched him reaching along the upper edges of the wall. Puzzled, she waited, then finally spoke.

"Josiah?"

"Faith! Your uncle happy with what we brought back?" Josiah turned, an easy smile coming to his face. He watched the emotions flickering across her face. He had already come to read them, even in just a day. She was definitely someone he wanted to get to know better.

She nodded. "He was. We were given much more than what we ordered."

"You deserved it. I know the owner; we were in college together. I also did his website. It wouldn't have mattered, though. He was not happy, to say the least, when he found out what had happened. It wasn't in him to let a good customer walk away like Pete wanted you to."

"I didn't think he was. Now, care to explain what's going on?"

Josiah shot her a glance, then stood back to stare up at the wall. "We have a problem here, and I need to talk to you and your uncle both."

Seth leaned against the work table, eyes on Josiah as he paced the room, gathering his thoughts.

"You've found something, Josiah. What is it?"

Josiah turned, watching Seth and then Faith. How did he tell them what he had found? Lord, if I were on speaking terms with You, this would be one time I would be. But I know You don't hear me, so there's no point, is there? He felt discomfort at the thought.

"I did. Running along the tops of the walls all around the building is a cable that shouldn't be there. It's not electrical or from your internet. I've sent a picture of it on to a friend, to see what he has to say about it. I have a feeling it's all related to what you're going through."

Seth nodded, lost in thought. "Jonathan mentioned the same thing, and a few nights later, his place went up in smoke."

Josiah nodded. "That's about what I thought. I've pulled it down and hidden it away for evidence. Did Faith mention that a friend's mother was coming to help tomorrow?"

Seth nodded, eyes watchful. "She did. You have wonderful friends, young man. Now about that wire?"

"If I can, I would like to put up a cot in here and stay in the building. I would also like to get that wire to my friend in Logan City."

Seth nodded, avoiding Faith's eyes. He knew they weren't done and Josiah's offer had come at the right time. "There's a cot in the room off this, Josiah. You're welcome to use it. There's also a small fridge if you want to store any food, but we'll be feeding you."

Later, Faith stared at the pattern she was to be putting together, her thoughts on what Josiah had found. Who placed that there, Lord, and when? It's not likely we'll ever find out though, will we? She started as a hand touched hers.

Josiah stood beside Faith, watching her face. He had no idea what her thoughts were but they seemed dark.

"What would you like me to do for you, Faith? We can get started on what we need to do today."

She nodded, her eyes tracing the pattern she had laid out. "I need the following sheets of glass gathered." She handed him a list. "I've always labeled the slots the glass is stored in. That should help."

"It will. While I'm doing this, pull up your website and I'll take a look at it today."

Hours later, Josiah sat back in his chair, stretching, watching from the desk he was seated at as Seth and Faith worked to place the pattern. How they had managed to cut so many pieces, he wasn't sure, but he could see the pain and fatigue lining her face. She's over done it, now hasn't she, he thought.

He rose, stretched again to loosen the kinks from his back and shoulders, then stood beside Faith as she stared once more at the pattern.

"This is nice, Faith." Josiah studied the sun catchers they had been working on. "How much cutting did you do?"

"Not a lot. With these, Uncle Seth can do a lot of it. We're in good shape with this order, I think."

"It's complete, Faith. We can wrap and get them ready to ship tomorrow." Seth stopped speaking, his eyes thoughtful. "But I can guarantee you they won't ship from here. They'll be delayed somehow."

"Not a problem, Seth. We'll figure out a way to get them to another town." Josiah stared down at his phone, thinking through who he could ask. "What is the absolute last day they need to ship?"

"Tomorrow."

"Then it happens. Package them first thing, and I'll make sure to get them mailed." He turned to Faith. "Now, about your website. I've found a lot of issues, not of your making I might say."

"So there was a problem." She was resigned. Lord, what else can go wrong?

"There were a few. I found where someone has tried to hack into it. I've emailed a friend for him to look into that. Don't worry, he's good. He's what you call an ethical hacker, hired to try and hack in to companies and websites to test their strength and vulnerability. He'll get back to me as soon as he can. I've taken down that website for now." He wouldn't tell her that it was her cousin, Noah, he had emailed.

"Josiah! That's our lifeline. How can we manage our orders without it?" Faith's voice had begun to raise by the time she finished.

Josiah caught her hand and led her to the computer, pushing her down into the chair. "Go ahead. Pull up your website."

She stared at him, green eyes full of anxiety. "But, you disabled it."

He shook his head. "The old one. Pull up your site."

She stared at him, then at her uncle. Finally, Seth nodded. She sighed, turning to the monitor, hoping that the website was still functional. The majority of their orders were done by mail, and they needed that website to generate those very orders.

Josiah stepped back, letting Seth stand behind her. A noise from the back door caught his ear, and with a quick look at the two, he moved to there and stepped outside, eyes scanning the area in the growing dusk. He turned, just as a blow from the side connected with his head, and he crumpled to the ground, head spinning before he dropped down into that well of darkness.

The dark form stood over him, then turned at a sound from behind him. He felt himself grabbed and dragged away, thrown into a vehicle, and then he too disappeared. A second figure stood over Josiah, shaking his head. What had this town come to? He looked around, then moved away. There was too much danger, he thought, to get involved.

Faith stared at the computer screen. How had Josiah managed to capture exactly what she wanted, without talking to her at all? She just knew it would bring more business, and that would be a problem, she thought. They could barely keep up now. Then, she spotted it.

"Uncle Seth, look!" She pointed to the banner of the website. "Look what he put in." She quoted the verses, prominent against a stained glass background. "Psalm 27:13-14 I remain confident of this: I will see the goodness of the Lord in the land of the living. Wait for the Lord; be strong and take heart and wait for the Lord."

"I see that, Child. He used your verses from Psalms you had on the other website. Now, why would he do that, when he doesn't appear to be following God?"

"It's because I had them there. I prayed that when we re-did the website, these would be front and centre. And they are." She spun in her chair. "Now, where'd he go?"

Seth looked around. "He was right behind me when we started looking at the site. You're right. Where is he?"

The two searched the building, then stared at one another. "Did he go outside, Uncle Seth? I didn't hear the door."

"That's something we need to rectify, Faith, both doors." Seth headed for the back door. "I want you to stay inside. It's getting dark, and I don't need someone coming after you."

Stepping outside, Seth stared around. Now where did that young fellow get to, he wondered? He knew he hadn't driven away, his truck was still there. As he walked forward, his foot struck something and he barely kept his balance. He started, then dropped to his knees beside Josiah, reaching to feel for a pulse. Strong and steady, he thought. Now, why is he lying down here? He rose back to his feet and struggled to lever Josiah over his shoulder. Thank God, he's alive.

Faith watched in horror as her uncle staggered back into the work room and then over to the cot, dropping Josiah down. Josiah's right arm flopped over the side of the bed before Seth tucked it back beside him.

"Bring me some warm water and a cloth, Faith, and then the first aid kit." He turned Josiah's head to face the light, wincing at the blow he must have taken.

Faith stood once more and watched as her uncle worked over Josiah. There was no way she would call the paramedics if she could help it, she thought.

Seth sat back and looked up at his niece. "He took a good blow to the head." He turned to stare back at the door. "I didn't hear anyone, so whoever it was must have left." He reached to dress the wound on the side of Josiah's head.

"We can't leave him here by himself tonight, Uncle Seth."

"No, we can't and we can't move him." Seth stood and paced, finally looking down at Josiah. "We have those air mattresses, Child. If they still inflate, we'll bunk here too. Let me go pull them out. You stay right here."

She nodded, watched as her uncle left, then sat on the edge of the cot, her eyes watchful, waiting for Josiah to rouse.

Chapter 5

Josiah stirred in the early morning, eyes blinking open, then closing again at the pain beating behind them. What had happened? He groaned softly as his hand found the sore spot on the side of his head. What had he run into? And what day was it? He heard soft steps, then felt a gentle hand moving his own hand back to his chest. Another hand slipped behind his head and raised it enough he could sip from the glass of water held to his mouth. Head back on the pillow, he waited for the room to stop spinning.

Faith watched as Josiah roused, concerned that it had been so long. She knew he'd have a brutal headache and her heart raised in prayer for healing for him. She glanced back at where her uncle slept. He hadn't roused when she had been up and down over the night. Frustrated with the sling she had been wearing, she had finally taken it off. The pain had been bad at first but had eased off, just as she knew it would. She would just have to be careful, that was all.

Her eyes strayed back to watch as Josiah once more slept. Who did this, Lord? Was it because he had helped us or was there something else? Knowing she wouldn't get any more sleep, she moved silently back to the work room and the orders that were waiting. She would work for a while, at least until the two men were awake.

Josiah pulled himself upright, holding his head in his hands as he perched on the side of the bed. The headache was much better, he thought. He looked up as he heard steps heading his way.

Faith stood and stared down at Josiah, assessing him in the morning light.

"Feeling better?" Her question was quiet.

He nodded, surprised that it didn't make his headache worse. "I am. The headache pretty much gone I would say."

"Uncle Seth gave you some of his special headache medicine last night. Don't worry, nothing in it could hurt you. It's herbs and that kind of stuff. Really works."

Josiah shoved his feet into his boots and stood, waiting for the dizziness to pass, and then moved towards the work room. "Thank you. I have no idea what happened. The last I remember is watching you pull up your website."

"And thank you for that. It's all I could dream and hope for. You've worked wonders there. We already have had numerous compliments on the site, and orders are coming in." She chewed on her bottom lip in a way he was coming to recognize.

"And you're worried you're not going to be able to fulfill the orders, given what's going on?"

She nodded, her eyes on his. "I am. It's coming to the point we need to hire but I'm really hesitant to bring someone in, given the situation."

"Tell you what. Talk to Bill's mom today when she gets here. She's been wanting to work, to help out their finances, but hasn't found what she wants to do. She loves working with her own stained glass projects. Hire her part-time for now. I can vouch for her."

Faith nodded, her thoughts not on what he was saying. "Who hit you, Josiah? And why? Is it because you're helping us?"

He shrugged. "I have no idea. That's what we're going to have to talk about." He watched as she opened her mouth to speak, laying his finger on it. "No, not right now. There's your uncle with our breakfast, and then we have to make plans to get your parcels mailed. I have a friend coming in this morning as well. He'll help us out."

Bill watched from the sidelines as Josiah stood talking with his mother, Beth, and Faith. Seth was finishing the packages, ready for the two younger men to head out with them. Bill approached him, thoughts running as to what had happened.

"Seth, talk to me. What's happening in your town?"

Seth looked up at him, then shook his head. "It's complicated, son. Tell you what, you hang around here long enough, you'll figure it out." Seth reached for a piece of paper and a pen, scribbling a note he held out to Bill.

Bill read it, and then raising his eyes, watched as Seth nodded.   He sighed, knowing he would have to talk to Josiah and that wouldn't be so easy.

Faith watched as Bill and Josiah spoke with her uncle and then turned to a third younger man who had entered. She didn't know this man, but Josiah and Bill did. She turned back as Beth questioned her on the design, missing the speculative glances both Bill and the new arrival threw her way.

"How do you want to do this, Josiah?" Samuel, friend to both men, asked, his eyes studying first his friend, then turning to Faith.

Josiah ran his hands through his hair, wincing at he hit the sore spot. "I'm sure we're being watched right now. We need to get those parcels out of here and to another town, but I have a feeling we'll be stopped before we get too far."

Bill nodded, then turned to count the parcels. "What is there, twelve, fifteen?"

Seth approached.   "There's eighteen there, Bill.   We package them in smaller cartons, just because of the weight. As you can see, the cartons are not that big." Seth was worried about involving Josiah and his friends.

Bill opened the back door and left, studying the vehicles parked there. He nodded, then returned to the three men. They listened to his plan, Seth protesting. Faith wandered over just at the end of the discussion.

"What did you fellows decide on?"

Josiah turned to her, watching the stress and strain showing on her face, and not liking it. He wanted to remove that from her. Bill and Samuel exchanged glances, a small smile on each face. Was she the one they had been praying for? But both knew that Josiah wasn't ready for anything like that. He had his own fights he had to resolve, one involving God.

"We have a plan that involves leaving you and Seth here with Bill's Mom. One of us is staying with you as well." Josiah met Seth's eyes and frowned at the look he surprised there. "The other two of us are taking off with the parcels."

Bill excused himself to take a call, then returned. "It's all set. As long as we have the parcels there by 11:00, we'll get them out today." He nodded at Seth and then stepped back out, opening the back of his SUV, ready to place the packages. Samuel and Josiah walked out the door with some of the cartons. The three men stood talking for a bit, then finished loading them. Bill waited until Josiah came back out.

"Are you sure about this, Josiah?"

Josiah stared into the distance, his eyes narrowing. "No, I'm not, Bill. We're being watched, you know. I haven't figured out who or why yet. Last night was a wake-up call. I didn't see anyone at all when I stepped outside. Neither did Seth. There were a number of footprints where he found me, but it's useless to call in the local police."

"I wondered if you had. I had a chance to talk with my lieutenant yesterday. He's heard talk and rumours over the years, but they've never had a complaint put into them or been asked to investigate." He looked around, his eyes watchful, not seeing anything. "Let's hit the road. We want to meet Jonah and Adam in thirty minutes. I pray this works."

Josiah nodded, not sure what he believed about prayer any more, having watched and listened to Faith and her uncle. Maybe what his friends had been saying to him over the years was finally making sense. But what did he do with it, given what he found himself in right now? He turned as Bill spoke.

"We have a tail, just like you figured."

Josiah turned to watch behind them, a frown on his face. "That's the car that followed Faith and I from the hospital, I think. What's going on?"

Bill shrugged and kept watch behind them. "I didn't tell you but a couple of friends from the force are waiting for us up ahead in their personal vehicles. They'll provide an escort to where we're meeting Jonah and Adam and then escort them in to Oak City."

Josiah stared at his friend. "And when did you arrange this?"

"Last night. We were out for a meal after patrol and they were asking about you. When they heard what was going on, they volunteered." He threw a quick glance at Josiah. "They've heard the same rumours and want to see the dirty ones taken down. What we can't figure out is who and how."

Josiah shrugged. "I have no idea. What I'm hearing from Seth and Faith is that it's only a couple so far, Brownlee for one. They have no idea how far up it goes."

Bill nodded. "It might be just Brownlee but I would think there's someone else. You say there's no evidence to prove anything?" Josiah nodded. "But there's evidence gathered?"

Josiah turned to watch in his mirror as two vehicles pulled up around them, one in front, the other behind. "Your friends, I take it? There is evidence gathered but it disappears and Brownlee claims there's no proof." Josiah hesitated, not wanting to shed suspicion on another person. "There's one person I wish I could investigate. There a physician at the hospital both Seth and Faith have had run-ins with. He wasn't happy that I was there for the two."

"What's his name?"

"Ted Watson, I think it was." At the silence from his friend, Josiah shot him a quick look. "What? Do you know him?"

Bill sighed, then nodded, as he signalled to make a turn. "Yeah, I do. Joanna had problems with a physician of that name a few years ago. She had to file for a restraining order against him." Bill's sister was a nurse and had worked in the hospital in Faith's town, until she had to move to get away from the gossip.

"Really? Then Faith may well be in danger without realizing it."

"She is. Stay as close as you can, Josiah. Only the Good Lord knows why He put you were He did, but that's where He wants you." Bill expected sarcasm and denial from Josiah. When none came, he gave a quick look and then pondered what was running over Josiah face. Is he finally reaching out to You again, Lord? Help him to find his way back to You. He and Josiah had been friends for years and it grieved him how Josiah had turned from God.

Pulling to a stop, Bill sat for a minute, then turned to Josiah. "I'll do what research I can, Josiah. If you can find anything he touched that's not disturbed, get it to me. I'll run it for evidence and prints."

Josiah turned to him, then reached into his pocket. "I found this that day when I was leaving the shop. I have no idea what it is."

Bill took the metal object, turning it over and over in his hands. "I've seen it before but I can't remember where. Can I take it?" At Josiah's nod, he reached to the glove compartment and pulled out a plastic bag and dropped the object into it. "I'll let you know what I find out," he stated as he tucked it into a shirt pocket.

Faith looked up a couple of hours later as the back door opened. She relaxed as she saw Josiah and Bill enter. Josiah nodded at her, then headed for the front of the shop, a grim look on his face. What was going on, she wondered? Bill spoke to his mother, then began searching the shop.

Faith turned to find her uncle standing beside her. She went to question him, but his hand on her arm stopped her. He pointed to the back door and she followed.

"What's going on, Uncle Seth?"

Seth stared around, not quite sure how he was going to explain what the men had discovered now.

"Uncle Seth?"

He sighed, then turned to face her. "Bill discovered cameras on the outside of the building. He and Josiah are searching inside now."

"Cameras? But wait! We don't have cameras in place."

"I know we don't. These are ones that would be spying on us, my dear. That's how they knew when and where to strike and to put up that cable."

Bill and Josiah stood talking together when the two re-entered the work room, then turned to watch Seth and Faith. Sighing, Seth walked towards them.

"What did you find, boys?"

Bill looked at him, then down at the box he held. "Cameras, listening devices, motion sensors that set the devices off. Someone really wanted to know what was going on in here."

Faith stared at him. "But why? We only do stained glass and ship that. We don't package until the day we ship, so no one could add anything to our packages."

"I can't tell you why, Faith, but for some reason, you have people monitoring what you do and don't do. We've found them all, I think. I've gone over your security set up and I'll have some recommendations for you."

Chapter 6

Faith watched as Beth drove away on Friday afternoon.   Thank you, Lord, for sending such a sweet lady to us. She fits in so well and is so eager to learn. We're ahead now, thank you, Lord. She turned as she felt someone standing beside her.

Josiah had watched over the week as Faith had started to relax as she and Beth had worked on the orders. He wanted to get to know her better, but he knew his stance on God would prevent that. He wanted that to change, but he didn't think it ever would. He just couldn't, or was it wouldn't, trust Someone he couldn't see or feel.

Faith watched the conflicting emotions cross Josiah's face, then spoke. "Has Bill any word on what he was investigating for you?"

Josiah grinned at her. "Who said he was investigating anything now?"

She gave an unladylike snort. "You're dreaming if you think I don't see the conversations you two are having."

Josiah nodded. "He hasn't got anything back yet, but he has a friend on the force here and has been talking to him. He says his friend isn't happy with the way the force is going under the current chief. There are a number of officers who feel the same. Bill thinks it's just a couple of individuals. When he has enough to take to his supervisor, he will."

"And how long will that be? How many more people are going to be hurt or lose everything in the meantime?" She watched as a car pulled in to the parking lot.

Josiah felt her withdraw and he turned to see who it was. "I take it you don't want to talk to him."

She shook her head, turning to head for the work room. "I have a restraining order against him. He's not supposed to be anywhere near me."

"Does he know that? He was active in your treatment at the hospital."

She stopped to stare at Josiah. "He couldn't have been. The doctors there know better."

"Go on in. I'll deal with him for you."

Josiah stepped into the pathway and waited for Ted Watson to approach him.

"Get out of my way!" Ted stopped in front of Josiah, expecting him to move.

"Not happening. I understand you have an order keeping you away from Faith."

Ted flipped his hand in the air. "That was a misunderstanding. I want to talk with her."

Josiah held up a hand. "Not a misunderstanding. So turn around and leave."

"And who gave you the right to tell me that?"

Josiah didn't answer, merely stared down the man in front of him. What do people see in him, he wondered? How did he ever make through to become a doctor?

Ted watched, then spoke again. "Get out of my way."

Josiah shook his head. "As I said, that's not happening. Faith has too many friends who won't put up with your tricks."

"What tricks?" The sneer covered Ted's face in an ugly manner.

"Joanna."

Ted stepped back at the spoken name. "What are you talking about?"

"I know that lady and her brother quite well. I suspect there are many more who should come forward and are too afraid to. So turn yourself around, get back in your car, and leave. If I hear of you even being within 500 feet of Faith, I'll have you arrested."

Ted glared at him, stared past him at the shop, and then turned on his heel, almost running to his car. Dust and gravel spewed in his wake at the speed with which he disappeared. Josiah watched, knowing it was far from over. Until someone was strong enough to come forward and confront him publicly, nothing would change. His fear was that the lady who would do that would be Faith.

He turned and found Faith standing behind him.

"What did you say to him?"

"Just told him to stay away from you and that if he didn't, I'd have him arrested."

"That won't happen in this town."

"It might not but if he approaches you at all, get away from him. Bill's sister had her own issues with him and finally had to move away."

"I remember her leaving. I always wondered what happened to her."

"He did. I didn't know that until the other day." He draped an arm over Faith's shoulders and turned her back to the shop. "Are you open on Saturdays?"

She nodded. "For a few hours. Tourists stop by and shop." She stopped, staring ahead of her. "I'm thinking that we need to re-vamp the showroom somehow."

"Then, tomorrow we'll work on that." He drew her forward, his arm still around her shoulders. "I have some work I need to do, but we'll work on your plans tomorrow. If you have some." He ducked the elbow she aimed at him, laughing with her.

Seth watched the two younger people walk his way, content with what he saw. *Please, Lord, bring him back to You. I can see the attraction between the two, but I know my Faith. It won't go anywhere until he does, and I feel certain he's the one You chose for her.*

"Uncle Seth, what say we pull out all the stops for supper tonight?" Faith's voice reached him, a cheerful note in it.

"Sounds good, Faith. You go ahead with Josiah. I want to go back over the orders."

Faith linked her arm with her uncle. "Not tonight, Uncle Seth. Tonight we relax."

Turning from his laptop the next afternoon, Josiah watched as Seth and Faith moved around merchandise in the shop, aiming for the best display. The debate had become heated at times, and he had smiled to himself. He glanced down at the screen at the website he had been working on. It was finished, he thought, and sent the information on to the client.

He pulled up his email program and flicked through his business emails. He sighed. He was getting more work than he could handle or even wanted. How did he ever cut back, he thought? He realized how tired he was getting, not just physically, but in all ways. So, Lord, are we going to be on speaking terms again? Is that why I'm in this small town? I've about reached the bottom of the barrel now, Lord.

He looked up as a hand touched his shoulder. Faith stood there, a puzzled look on her face.

"Josiah, are you all right?"

He nodded, pushing back his chair and standing. "It's always a sad moment but happy moment when I finish a website for a client." He paused as he looked back at the screen and then sat back down.

"What's this?" he murmured, pulling up an email.

Faith gasped as she saw it. "Josiah, that's Bill. Isn't that when he pulled us over?"

Josiah nodded grimly. "It is. We were followed. This looks as if it's a still shot, taken from behind Bill's car somewhere, or from the other side of the road."

The photo showed Josiah and Bill talking outside the truck, Faith watching from the interior.

Josiah read the email, an email warning that retribution was coming and that if they cooperated, it wouldn't happen.

"I'm going to send this on to Bill. He'll have someone look into it for us. And it's interesting that it came to my work email, not yours. Whoever it is has to know who I am."

Seth looked up from where he had been working with a customer, a look on his face that said explanations would come later.

Josiah sighed, knowing that whatever was going on was far from over. Who is it? And why? Just protection money or is it something more sinister? He had felt the chill in the town when he was downtown that morning, not a chill from the temperature, but a chill from fear and anxiety. How many people are paying, Lord, he questioned, not even realizing that he was again speaking to God?

Looking around in a worried manner, Faith spoke in a quiet voice, "We're not done, are we, Josiah? He's still out there, isn't he?"

Josiah looked around, then stood, pushing Faith down into his chair. "He is. We'll have to take precautions with you two and your shop. Bill's coming through late Monday afternoon to update your security system. He's bringing motion sensor cameras as well for the outside and strong motion sensor lights. He's also bringing them for your home."

"Will that help?"

"We hope it will. Nothing's guaranteed, though. You need to take as many precautions as you can. One of those is that you're never alone, if you can help it."

Startled eyes flew to study his. "What do you mean?"

"Just that. If they catch you on your own, who knows what will happen. Look what happened when you were with your uncle." He looked around. "Now, about your orders. What needs to be shipped on Monday?"

"There's a stack back in the shop ready to go. There's quite a few, actually." She stood and headed that way, stopping as she heard the door open. A gasp was drawn from her body.

Josiah spun, staring at the man who had entered, eyes narrowing as he assessed him. He could feel the tension radiating from Faith's body.

"Chief Brownlee! What can we do for you?" Faith's voice was tinged with frost as she spoke.

Josiah moved to stand behind her, his hands on her shoulders. He found feel her leaning back towards him.

"Just making sure you're all safe, Faith." His eyes were cold as was his voice.

"As you can see, we are, Chief. Is there anything else?"

The Chief watched her for a moment. Then his eyes raised to Josiah, narrowing as he read the challenge there. He finally nodded and turned and walked away.

Josiah frowned, trying to determine exactly what had just happened.

Seth spoke from behind him. "What did he want, Faith?"

She shrugged, looking around Josiah at her uncle. "He said to make sure we're safe. Was that genuine concern or a threat?"

Seth stared at the door, then spoke. "I would say a threat. It's been a changed town in the last four years since he took over as chief, and not in a good way."

Faith moved away to stare out the door. "That is has, Uncle Seth."

Josiah looked between the two. "Brownlee. Any relation to the officer who did nothing?"

Seth started to laugh at Josiah's description. "That's perfect, Josiah. And yes, he's the officer's father." Seth paused, lost in thought. "Everyone in town is still trying to figure out how he got to be chief. He certainly wasn't the most qualified or even the most liked."

Josiah nodded, knowing he would be asking someone to research him. "Now, what? You're closing, right?"

Faith nodded as she locked the doors and flipped the sign to read closed. "We are.

It's been a long week." She headed for the front counter and closed off the cash register, tucking the cash and money into a locked bag.

"Tell me you don't keep that here in the store or in your home." Josiah walked towards her, finger pointed at the bag.

Faith stopped, startled. "No, we have a safe we keep it in until we do the bank run on Monday. No one would find it."

"Don't bet on that, Faith. If they really want to find it, they will."

Faith laughed, then grabbing his hand, pulled him to the work room. "The cameras you found didn't point at where we have the safe." She reached to pull out a section of the counter running along the showroom wall and revealed a built-in safe. She stashed the money bag inside, locked it again and shoved the counter back in place.

"That's interesting. Did you put it in or was it already here?"

"We put it in." Faith turned to scan the work room. "It looks as if all is set for Monday."

Chapter 7

    *F*aith watched as Josiah moved nervously the next morning. She had asked him to come to church with them, and already she could tell he was very uncomfortable. She reached for his hand and he stilled, his eyes turning to her.

"They're not going to expect you to do anything, you know." She had a grin on her face as she said that. "You don't even have to participate if you don't want to."

Josiah nodded. "It's not that, Faith. I can feel someone watching us."

"You're sure? Here in church?"

He took a quick look around. "Yes, here in church. Not everyone who goes to church practices what they hear all week. There are a lot of Sunday morning Christians out there." He looked up as the police chief and his son passed by them, sending both Josiah and Faith a hard unreadable look. Josiah tilted his head at them. "Like those two."

Faith sighed. "I know what you mean. I'm just glad you're here with me today. Uncle Seth would be sitting with us if he wasn't at the door greeting." She froze as her eyes caught movement behind them. Turning, she looked around but couldn't see what had caught her attention.

Josiah watched as she looked around, then turned himself once more to scan the area. He sighed. He would have no idea what to look for, now would he, he thought to himself. Someone would have to hit him over the head and they had already tried that. His attention was drawn back to the front of the church as the worship band started up. This was different, he thought. Not at all what he had been used to and not what he expected at all.

He listened to Faith's pure alto singing the choruses and watched her face and movements. He wished he had that faith. His eyes were drawn to the plain rugged cross at the very front of the church. Lord, where do I go from here? How do I get back to where You are?

Faith turned to Josiah at the end of the service, waiting for him to speak. When he didn't, she tilted her head to watch him, catching movement from the far side of the church. Looking up, a frown crossed her face. Who was that who was watching them? She didn't know the man. He was a stranger to her but he looked familiar.

Josiah drew a deep breath and stood, looking down at Faith. "Tell me, Faith, what do you usually do on Sundays?"

She shrugged. "It's a day of rest for us. Uncle Seth and I tend to disappear for the day, each to our own amusements."

"Is that so?" Josiah looked up to see Seth watching him and giving him a nod. "So, would you be willing to spend it with me? I need to go back to my place and grab some stuff."

She shrugged. "Sure, why not? Any chance we can drop in on Noah?"

He shook his head as they made their way to his truck. "No. He's overseas, in London, I think he said."

"It would have been nice to see him. He hasn't been home in a few months."

Later that afternoon, Faith spun, startled as a voice sounded from the door, a towel she was folding clasped in her hands.

"Josiah! You're back, man! When did you get in?" The man entering stopped, startled to see Faith standing there, surprise in his eyes. "You're not Josiah!"

Faith watched, trying to control her smile, laughter in her eyes, as he stepped back to check out where he was.

"Yep. Josiah's apartment, but you're definitely not him!" He stared at her as she struggled to control her laughter, biting her lip to do so. "So, where is he?"

"Right behind you, Zeke." Josiah slapped him on the shoulder as he moved past him. "Faith, this person trying to take his foot out of his mouth is our friend, Ezekiel, commonly known as Zeke."

Faith laughed at that. "Yes, definitely a foot moment. Hi!"

Zeke glared at Josiah, then turned back to Faith. "Nice to meet you." He tilted his head. "Have we met?"

She shook her head. "No, I don't think so. I'm sure I would remember you." Her eyes moved to Josiah as he choked back laughter.

"She's Noah's cousin, Zeke."

"Noah's cousin? Now, I'm really glad to meet you. But what are you doing with this guy?" His thumb pointed at Josiah.

"He's been helping my uncle and I out for the last week at our glass shop."

"That's the cousin and uncle. Man, I need to get out there to see your work. Noah brags about you two all the time."

"Yeah, you do need to, Zeke." Josiah moved to pick up the bag he had set near the kitchen doorway of his apartment.

"You moving out, Josiah?"

"No. I'm staying with Noah's people for now." Josiah and Zeke stared at one another. Then Zeke nodded. "Don't worry, I'm not moving out."

"What else do you need to take out?" Zeke looked around.

"Just a couple of boxes from the office, Zeke, if you could. Faith, we'll be right back."

She laughed. "I'm sure you will be. Any more of your friends dropping in?"

Zeke broke out into laughter. "She's good, Josiah."

Faith walked towards the two men standing talking by Josiah's truck. She hesitated, not wanting to intrude, and was surprised when Josiah reached for her, an arm around her holding her close to him, Zeke eyeing the two of them.

"Did you say the property is right on the edge of town?"

Josiah nodded. "It is, but there's something strange there. I checked out the county maps. It's reading that the property is in the county, not the town."

Zeke stared into the distance. "I can remember when the county took back some of the town land, probably fifteen years ago. If you're right, then you can talk to Bill and have his supervisor start an investigation." Zeke looked down at Faith. "Does she know?"

"Do I know what?" Faith's eyes bounced between the two men.

"I did some research last night, Faith, and need to talk to both you and your uncle. Your property is not in the town. It's actually in the county." He tightened his hold on her as she moved. "That means you've been paying taxes to the wrong place. It also means that the town police can't investigate what happened to you and your property. County has to do that."

Faith relaxed back against Josiah. "Is this true? Does this mean we can finally get some answers?"

Zeke nodded. "It does. The police have to have known this. I'm to have dinner with Bill and his sister tonight. I'll have him call you."

"Please do."

A few more words, and Zeke moved away, the two watching him walk away.

"Is this really true, Josiah?" Faith hadn't moved away from him, feeling safe for the first time in months while his arm surrounded her.

"It is, Faith. Now, we'll need to get you some legal advice. A friend of mine, Samuel, is a title searcher. I sent him an email, asking him to do some research for me. The more information we have, the better stand we have."

"Why, Josiah?" She turned to look at him.

"Why? Because you need justice done, not just for the past fifteen years, but for what it is you've been put through. Because I care about you, Faith, in a way I've never cared about anyone before." Josiah studied her face, catching a look in her green eyes. "Don't worry, Faith. I'm not asking anything of you at this point beyond friendship."

She nodded. "Thank you, Josiah. You are struggling right now, but I sense that today, you're moving back towards God."

He stared into the distance, a look on his face that she recognized as one finding a treasure where he least expected it. "I am. You're a big part of my healing. That cross at the front of your church. It's different. It's not the smooth, polished crosses you usually see."

She shook her head. "No, it's not. A deacon in the church made it out of two trees, rugged and worn. His comment was that Christ wouldn't have hung on a polished cross."

"He's right, you know." Josiah turned to open the truck door and tucked Faith inside. Sliding behind the wheel, he spoke again. "No, I always imagined a rough, rugged cross." He paused again. "I've been so lax, Faith. I walked away from God in my teens when my Dad was stricken with cancer. He's still here and is after me all the time to come back to God." He turned to look at her, and she could see tears close to the surface. "He'll be glad to hear that I'm making my way back. He'll want to meet the lady who challenged me to do so."

She nodded, not quite sure how to respond.

"Uncle Seth, where are you?" Faith went looking for her uncle as Josiah moved his belongings into the room he had been using.

Seth raised his head from the book he had been reading. "Right here, Faith. Having a good day?"

"I am. And you?" At his nod, she linked arms with him and drew him towards the shop. "Josiah needs to talk with us. He's found out some interesting information for us. We can get the county police to investigate the incidents we've had."

"But how? We're in the town." Seth stared at his niece, then at Josiah.

"No, actually you're not and haven't been in fifteen years. The county took back part of the land and from what I can see, you're at least a mile inside the county lines."

"What! And the town has just been sending us tax bills for all this time?"

Josiah nodded. "I have asked a friend of Noah's and mine to do a title search on your property. He'll get back to me as soon as he can. Bill will be talking with his supervisor and asking that they investigate the incidents and the assault on Faith. Brownlee has to have known he couldn't."

Seth turned, running his hands through his graying hair, and paced. "This changes it all, doesn't it?" He stopped, paling. "That means we'll have to come up with the tax money for the county."

Josiah shook his head. "I don't think so. The town has been collecting illegally from you for all those years. They'll be responsible for reimbursing the county. If they don't, then we'll find you a lawyer to take them on. I don't think they'd want it coming out in the press what they've been doing or how lax their law enforcement has been."

A thud at the front door had them turning that way. Josiah headed that way, motioning for Seth and Faith to stay where they were. He couldn't see anyone as he looked out. He headed back through the work room to the back door, admonishing the two to stay where they were. He stopped as he approached the front, staring around, trying to get a sense of what had gone on. He couldn't see anyone but he could feel the presence of evil all around him. He could feel the eyes watching him. Approaching the front door, he stopped once more. What was going on, he wondered, staring at the bag that was moving?

Cautiously, he bent and picked up the package, hearing a faint meow. A cat, he thought? Who would leave a cat here like this?

He unzippered the bag, being cautious on opening it. A small kitten peeked up at him, the little black and white face catching at his heart. He cradled it to his chest as he searched the bag, finding nothing else.

He turned and once again stared around. What was going on, Lord? Who did this? And I guess we're back on speaking terms, Lord. It's been a long time. Heal my heart and aid me as I work to help Faith and Seth.

Chapter 8

𝒯aith watched as the little kitten played with Josiah's sneaker laces, tumbling around his foot. He reached down and scooped the kitten up, cradling her in his arm as he continued to work. Faith had named the little black and white kitten, Georgia, as she said she had a huge curiosity that would get her into trouble one day. She turned as she heard voices as the back door opened and Bill and another man in uniform entered.

"Faith, this is Lieutenant Andrew Jones. He's here to talk to you about what's been going on. I've told him what I know."

The senior police officer assessed the woman standing in front of him and then glanced at Josiah, who had come to stand behind her. Bill is right, he thought. Josiah has found his lady.

"Miss Lockwood, let me say I'm sorry for what you've been going through. If I had known that your property was in the county, we would have been investigating as soon as we knew."

"Thank you, sir. None of us knew until Josiah did some research." She turned to look at Josiah. "And I still haven't figured how he knew to research that."

Josiah shrugged. "I have no idea why I did. I was looking for a map to put with a website for a company in the county and happened to see your store on it. That map showed the county lines."

"I'm glad you did, Josiah. Now, maybe we can get to the end of what's going on." Seth had moved to stand near Faith. "Andrew, it's good to see you again."

"Seth. You're looking good." Andrew looked around the work room, then moved into the store out front. "Who's the artist? Faith? My goodness, girl, you have a real talent here. I understand Bill's mom has been helping you out. Good."

He turned back to face them. "Okay, then. Let's hear what's been going on and I mean everything, even if you think it's not important." He stopped speaking as he felt something around his feet and looked down. "Where did this kitten come from?"

"Josiah found her in a bag at the front of the store late yesterday. Just the bag and Georgia, nothing else."

"I kept the bag, Bill, just in case." Josiah pointed to where he had set it out of the way.

Bill nodded. "We'll take it with us."

Thirty minutes later, Andrew tucked his notepad away. "I think we have everything we need now, Faith and Seth. I'll certainly be in touch with the town police for the evidence that was gathered."

Faith snorted, causing them all to stare at her. "Do you really think they still have it?"

Andrew sighed. "I certainly hope they do. If not, I'll be taking it further."

They all looked towards the store as the bell rang. Josiah, standing near the door, looked behind him and tensed.

"Chief Brownlee. What can we do for you?"

"Just following up, Silverthorn. Are Faith and Seth here?"

Josiah stepped back to let him walk into the work room, where he stopped staring in anger at Andrew. "What are you doing here? This is town business."

Andrew shook his head. "Actually, Brownlee. It's not. It's county. This property has been part of the county for over ten years, close to fifteen if I remember correctly. Your police force shouldn't be involved in anything here. By the way, I understand there was evidence gathered when Faith was assaulted. You'll be getting the paperwork tomorrow to have it sent on to our offices."

"What evidence? There wasn't any collected."

Josiah spoke, his eyes staring at the chief. "There was. I was here when it was done. Perhaps you need to speak with your son and find out where he put it."

"What do you mean? If there was evidence, it'll be entered into our system."

Bill spoke up. "That's not what we've been told. We asked for it today and were told there was no evidence, but we know he collected it.”

The chief glared at the two other officers. “We’ll see about that.” He brushed by Josiah, knocking into his shoulder, as he moved quickly to leave the room.

“Well, that went well.” Faith’s droll comment broke through the silence, driving the men to laughter.

“That it did, Faith.” Andrew studied the three of them, Bill watching as well. “This is far from over. Somehow, you’ve made an enemy here in town. Watch your backs.” He pointed towards the door. “He may be the police chief, but he has a mean and angry streak, always has had.” He shook his head. “I still don’t know how he made to chief.” He turned and walked from the room, Bill following him.

Faith stared at the closing door, then at her uncle. “Now what, Uncle Seth? Where do we go from here?”

Seth shrugged. “Only the good Lord knows, Faith, Child. Let’s get back to work. Beth is due in tomorrow, isn’t she? You promised her some new designs to work with. Are they done?”

She sighed. "Not quite. I'm having trouble with my inspiration today."

Seth shared a look with Josiah and then nodded. He turned and walked away, leaving Josiah staring after him, mouth partly open. What just happened here, he wondered?

"Faith, come on. You need to get away." He reached out a hand.

"No, I don't. I need to work."

"When is the last time you took time off from here, other than a few hours here and there, and on Sundays?" He watched as she shrugged. "You're getting stale. You need to get out and find some new inspiration. Come on. Let's run away for the day. Seth can manage the shop."

She shook her head at him and then took his hand, letting him lead her out of the building and tuck her into his truck.

"Where are we heading, Josiah?"

"A place I like to go and think. It's a nature walk, not far from here in fact." He turned. "I'm sorry. I should have asked if you wanted to, not dragging you out of there."

"In case you didn't notice, you didn't have to drag too hard." She turned to look behind her. "We have no tails today, no one wanting to hurt us?"

"Not that I've seen." Josiah pulled into a parking spot at a local conservation area. "I found this spot a few years ago. When I feel overwhelmed or am trying to work out a design that just won't come, I walk through here, watching nature. It helps me to relax and get my thoughts straight."

An hour later, Josiah handed Faith a bottle of water as they sat on a rock near the river. He could see the relaxation and peace in her face.

"Thank you, Josiah, I needed this." Faith leaned back on her hands, face turned up to the sun.

"I did too. Thanks for coming"

They sat for a while, conversation quiet, the sound of the river mixing with their words.

A sudden noise behind them had Josiah rising. A shove sent him face first to the ground, where a knee rested between his shoulder blades and a forearm pushed against his neck. He struggled but was unable to dislodge his assailant. A hand grasped his wrist and twisted his arm behind his back. Hauled to his feet, arm still behind him, he desperately searched for Faith. She was held, a man's hand across her mouth and an arm binding her arms to her side. She had struggled, he could tell.

"What do you want?" He glared at the third man standing there. With hoodies raised and dark sunglasses on, he couldn't distinguish much about their faces. He noted they had bandanas around their lower faces.

"We don't want to hurt you, but we need to talk to you."

"Like this? Hidden behind disguises? Really?" Josiah flinched as his arm was forced higher behind his back. Cool it, he thought. Getting hurt won't get us out of this.

"We have a reason for being hidden. We need to speak to both of you and can't come openly to do that." The third man once again spoke, then nodded at the other two men.

Faith flew to Josiah's side when she was released and he wrapped an arm around her.

"What do you want to talk to us about?"

No words were said, but they were forced to walk back towards the parking lot, then directed down a separate path, coming to a hidden cabin. Faith frowned, not recognizing it and she thought she knew all the cabins in the area.

Shoved down on the dusty, musty couch, Josiah wrapped an arm around Faith again and kept her close to his side, his eyes watchful as the three men conversed away from them, their voices quiet. Quick glances were thrown their way. Josiah's eyebrows drew together in a frown. What was going on?

The door opened behind them and they heard someone else enter. Faith shifted closer to Josiah, who stared at the three men standing in front of them. The fourth man made no sound, but Josiah picked up that he was the leader of the men.

"So, you wanted to talk. What about?"

They heard a sigh from the man who had spoken to them earlier.   He looked behind them and then nodded.

"We're not your enemy.   We don't want to hurt you.   But we need to talk to you, particularly you, Faith, as a business owner in town."

"But, I'm not.   We've found out my business isn't in the town, but in the county."

The man nodded.   "We know that. We've known that for a quite a while. So do the men who are going from business to business collecting money."

"Protection money."   Josiah finally spoke. "How many have paid?"

"Too many.   Even one is too many. We're trying to bring them down and we need your help."

"And have what happened to Jonathan happen to us?   They've already assaulted Uncle Seth and I."   Faith was almost in tears. "What do you want?"

"We need you to help us bring these fellows done. We have a good idea who the leader is.   There are only two in town who are involved. They hire in their muscle when they need to.”

“And they make the evidence of crime disappear, don’t they?” Josiah stared at the men standing in front of him, somehow knowing he wouldn’t be able to turn to see who was behind him.

“We’ve heard rumours of that. It wouldn’t surprise us if that’s what they did.”

“Tell us why we should help you.” Faith’s voice was quiet, a question in it. Something about the men seemed familiar but she wasn’t sure at all any more about who she could or couldn’t trust in town.

The man who had been speaking stared behind them, then nodded. “We know we need to give you information about us, but we have to be cautious. This isn’t just about protection money. There’s a lot more going on in town that no one would ever suspect.

“The protection money could be directed at all the businesses, but it is something directed primarily at the arts-type of business. We’re a tourist destination, unlike some of the towns around us. If our artists pack up and move away, it destroys a base we have in our town. Rumours are going around that some of thinking of doing just that. We want to prevent that." He turned to Faith. "That's where you come in. So far, you and Jonathan have been the only ones we know of that have stood up to them. Andrew's in plans to rebuild his pottery workshop. We know they've been after you, Faith. We heard what happened to you. Josiah, you're what we need."

Josiah spoke up. "I'm not law enforcement. I don't do martial arts. I'm a web designer, not someone used to fighting someone."

A finger was pointed at him. "That's what we want. We want a website set up, where people can get information of what's happening and where they can report crimes, on an anonymous basis. Our police force is not totally corrupt, just a few and we're working on those names. We're not a vigilante group. Rather we're a group of concerned business people, wanting to bring peace and unity back to our town. We're drawn from diversity across the businesses in town."

"I still don't see what you want us to do." Faith was genuinely puzzled.

"We would like Josiah to set up our website so affected business will have a place they can go to. We'll provide him with the information that he needs to do so. It's not without risk, though, Josiah. If you can't or won't become involved, we understand." He turned to Faith, who had been trying to determine who was speaking and hadn't been able to. "It's also dangerous for you and your uncle. Whether or not people realized your business is not part of the town or not, they've proven they'll come after you. This won't change."

Josiah stared down at Faith, not willing to have her put at risk, but knowing that sometimes someone had to stand up to a bully and corruption. Faith turned her head to look up at him. Her eyes searched his face.

Without looking away, she spoke. "I'll do my part. I know Uncle Seth will as well. Josiah will need to make his own decision on that."

"I'm in, if Faith is." Josiah missed the looks the four men exchanged and the nod from the man behind, who somehow had known the two would agree to help.

The man exchanged glances with the other three, then quietly stepped from the cabin, pulling down his hoodie and pulling off the dark glasses and bandanna. His eyes raised to the sky, he prayed for protection for the two inside, for wisdom for their group as they sought to weed out the corruption in their town and to find those willing to fight back. It would have to be in God's strength that they fought. It was an unseen enemy they were after and like knights of old, they would have to buckle on their armour to fight back. He stood for a moment, breathing in the fresh scents of the forest, listening to the chatter and songs of the birds, the croaks from the frogs in the nearby creek, feeling the warmth of the sun filtering down through the branches. He missed this. Someday, he vowed, he would move back to this town but the timing wasn't right, not yet.

Chapter 9

$\mathcal{R}$eturned to his truck, Josiah and Faith watched as the men walked back into the forest the way they had just come. Josiah frowned, looking down at the papers he had been handed. *What did I get myself into? Lord, I guess when I asked if we were back on speaking terms, I meant it. I have no idea where to go with this. But Mom always maintained that You had a plan and purpose for us that we never knew about. You're going to have to be the guiding One in this.*

"Did that really just happen, Josiah?" Faith's voice was quiet as he tucked her into his truck.

Sliding behind the wheel, he stared out the front window. "It did. I'm not sure if we should have agreed to be involved."

Faith reached to grasp his forearm, causing him to look at her. "Sometimes, someone has to do what needs to be done. This time, it's us. Only, I have no idea where it's headed. And I have no idea what Uncle Seth will say. He would likely tell me that we're in a battle of good versus evil and that we needed to get our armour on, that the war is won, but we need to battle on."

"He would have agreed, I think." Josiah started the truck and backed out of the parking spot, heading back to Faith's shop.

Seth stared at the two of them as they explained in detail what had happened, his thoughts going back to days long ago when this very same thing had been fought through and won. He sighed to himself. Not again, Lord, please not again. I'm getting too old to be fighting like this. And I don't want to see these two hurt, and that's what happens when you fight back against this type of corruption.

"A website, you say, Josiah?" At Josiah's nod, he paused, studying the younger man standing tall and strong in front of him. "You remind me of myself years ago. Faith, you never knew, but when you were just young, your father and I had to fight this type of thing through. I hate to see that it's come back. This time, though, it's more insidious and from what you say, affecting all businesses in town. We just had a few affected when we fought it."

Faith stared at her uncle. "Dad and Mom never said a word. Nor did you."

"It was in the past, Faith. It would have served no purpose to bring it up." He paced the work room, deep in thought. "Now, that I think of it, it's always been around. I've heard vague rumours over the years." He stopped, his back to them, shoulders slumped. "And it always means someone gets hurt in the crossfire." He spun, eyes haunted. "I just don't want it to be you. Not like your father or Noah's father."

"Uncle Seth, what haven't you told Noah and I?"

He sighed again, then nodded at the stools around the work table. "Sit. Let me just say that it wasn't a pleasant time. Noah's father stood up to them and was critically injured. He lived for a couple of years, then died from those injuries. You know that Noah and his mother struggled for years to survive. Your own father and mother worked hard to support both their family and Noah's." He stopped, eyes sliding closed. "I have always wondered about that plane crash that took your parents and Noah's mother, whether there was more to it than what was said."

"Uncle Seth!" Faith's hand flew to her mouth. "Are you saying you think someone killed them?"

Tortured eyes met hers, then raised to Josiah. "That's what everyone has wondered, Faith. We can't prove anything now, it's been too long."

"Maybe not, but we can try. I know someone who might be able to help us out." Josiah's hand rested on Faith's. "If you have the information, I'll send it on to her."

"Her?"

Josiah nodded. "She's quite good, can find information no one else can. I'll see what she comes up with."

A week later, Josiah looked up from his computer and watched as Faith studied the pattern she was laying out. Beth worked quietly on the other side of the table, humming to the music playing from the CD. He tilted his head to listen, then smiled. Worship songs, he thought they were called. No wonder it was such a peaceful place to work. He had felt his heart healing, the stress melting away, and peace filling him once more. The passion for his work was back, but in a different way. He was no longer driven to make the money in the way he had been. He wanted to change what he worked on but wasn't even sure how he could.

He stared back at his screen. He had been working on the website for the men who had talked with them. He snorted to himself. No, he thought, abducted them to talk with them. As promised, they had given him all the information he had asked for. He had set up a separate email just for them to contact him. He knew he could have it traced back, but something kept him from doing that.

"Josiah, is that the website?" Faith peeked over his shoulder. "Wow! Have they approved it?"

He nodded. "They have. I'm still finalized the little details, but it should work." He had set up a website designed to draw in the businesses in town, having been asked to make it easy to follow and encrypted for the businesses so that it couldn't be hacked. He had one final step to do and he wasn't even sure he should. Something kept him back from asking Noah to try and hack into it. "I need to see if someone can hack into it."

"Noah?"

He shook his head. "No. I want to keep him out of it, if I can. I know others who could do that. It's a matter of who I can trust to do that." He sat back, then drawing up his own website, sent a quick email off. "He'll get back to me when he can."

"Not to change the subject, but have you heard anything back on the plane crash?"

He shook his head. "No. She's still working on it for me. She's been dealing with some personal stuff from what I'm told. Someday, I'd like you to meet her."

"Girlfriend, Josiah?"

He spun in his chair, catching the uncertain look on her face. He shook his head. "No, Faith. I wouldn't do that to you. I want to get to know you better, and we're working on that, given what we're going through. No, she's a friend as is her husband."

Faith stared at him, eyes round at his word. "You do?" At his nod, she smiled. "Well, then, I guess if she's a friend and married, that's the way it is."

He shook his finger at her as he laughed, then sobered as he heard voices from the store. He rose and walked quietly to the door, watching as the large man moved among the displays, Seth watching from the counter.

"I would hate to see your niece's work destroyed, man. But you understand that we need to come to terms. Business terms you know." The man looked up as Josiah stepped into the room. "And bringing in muscle won't change that."

"I'm not muscle, you know." Josiah's eyes narrowed as he took in the man. "A friend who's helping out. And I would advise you and your bosses to stay away from us. We're not part of the town you're trying to take over. Haven't been in years."

The man stared at him before pacing closer, getting right into Josiah's face. A finger stabbed at his chest, inflicting pain that Josiah did his best to hide. "You are, if we say so."

Josiah shook his head, not backing down. "Nope, we're not. We're outside the town limits. So your little protection scheme won't work for you here. Besides, smile for the camera. We have your face on file now."

The man doubled a fist, raised it, then thought better. "We're not done, Lockwood. Not by a long shot." He turned and strode angrily from the room.

"I don't know if you should have done that, Josiah. He'll be back and we'll be out of business."

Josiah shook his head. "Not yet! They build up fear in people, escalating as they go along." He looked around the show room. "What I would suggest is this."

He made suggestions to both Seth and Faith, meeting every one of their protests with reasons and plans.

Faith finally stepped back, studying the changes they had made. "I don't like this, Josiah."

"I know you don't, but think about it. Most of your sales are done online. Keeping your wares under lock and key makes sure you have what you need to sell that way. Photos here are not out of place. You don't get a lot of walk-in clients right now. I pray that by the time the tourist season really starts you can put your wares back out."

Seth drew his niece to his side, an arm wrapped around her. "He's right, Faith. As much as we want to provide a good variety for people to see, we have to take precautions against these men."

Josiah walked away, torn in his desire to stay and comfort the two, but needing to find some space to deal with what he had to. God, where are you? Why are they going through this? Don't you even care?

He felt a hand on his shoulder. Beth stood beside him.

"It's a hard row you undertaken, Josiah. Seth told me what you're up to. I'm in all the way, as is Bill. Bill's father, Will, is too, if he can help. Bill will be around here when he can. He has a friend on the force here who'll be stopping by as well. They're both thinking that Seth and Faith need to expand their shop and they're working on a way for that to happen and to provide you with an office here."

He turned, studying the older woman. "What do you mean?"

"We can see how you feel about Faith. You're not moving back to Oak City, my boy. Your heart's here." She turned as a commotion broke out from outside the store.

Josiah hit the back door on a run and ran for the front of the building, sliding to a stop. Now what, he thought, as he studied the crate sitting right in the middle of the driveway. He cautiously approached it, not seeing anything that would tell him what it was.

Seth appeared at his side. "What is this?"

"I have no idea, Seth, but I don't like it, not given what you just went through."

He pulled out his phone, just as Bill approached from the other side.

"What do you have here, Seth?"

"That's what we're trying to determine, Bill. I was just about to call it in. We had another run in with that man again today. Now this."

Bill walked around the crate. "I'm not sure what this it, but let me call in someone to take a look at it." He stopped, his eyes scanning the surrounding area. "I would suggest we all move inside. Someone's watching us."

They watched as the bomb unit examined the crate and then opened it, staring first at what was inside and then back at the shop. Josiah stepped outside with Seth at Bill approached them.

"There's no bomb, thankfully, Seth, Josiah but I think you both need to see what's inside before we talk to Faith." He paused, then handed over an envelope to Bill. "This was dropped off at the station for you today, Josiah. I said I'd bring it out." He took a look at the brown envelope with animal tracks all over it. "Interesting envelope."

Josiah gave a half laugh. "Weird sense of humour too, she has. Now, about the crate."

"You won't like it, Josiah. Nor you, Seth." Bill watched as the two men moved forward, stopping at the crate and staring down.

Josiah spun, a look of horror on his face. "It's a coffin, Bill!"

Bill walked towards him, nodding. "It is. It's a warning, Josiah. They'll kill all three of you if you don't play nice with them. And I know you well enough to know you won't." He stared past them as Andrew walked towards them. "So, how do we keep you three safe?"

Josiah shook his head. "I have no idea. I really thought they would back away when they found out we weren't part of the town."

"They won't." Andrew spoke from beside him. "They'll use you as an example to the other businesses that even changing addresses won't work." He stared around, feeling the eyes watching them. "They're here, watching for your response. They expect to see fear and dismay. Are you going to oblige them?"

Seth turned to Andrew, then looked towards the shop. "I say, no, but we need to keep Faith safe. How do we do that?"

Bill turned as well to face the shop. "I've some ideas that way, but I need to talk to Andrew as well before I say anything." He turned as he heard a familiar voice calling him.

"Hey, Hillbilly! What are you doing here?" A tall thin man walked his way.

"Stringbean! How are you? Just the man I wanted to see."

"I am? Seth called about his new building. You planning on building, too?"

Josiah's eyes bounced between the two men. Long time friends, he figured, but the names they called one another!

"Josiah, this is Cyrus Greene. We call him Stringbean. He's never liked Cyrus."

The man groaned. "Just don't tell my mother that, please, Hillbilly." He turned to Seth. "What are you planning, Seth?"

Seth shook Cyrus' hand. "We would like to expand the work shop, revamp the show room, and put in some office space as well as classroom space. Faith has always wanted to hold classes to teach her art."

Stringbean walked around the existing building, and then through it. Josiah watched him, then turned to watch the two officers as they conferred with the bomb squad leader. He walked towards them, leaving Seth to find Stringbean. Faith watched from the doorway of the shop, her eyes following first Josiah and then turning to her uncle.

"Uncle Seth? What's going on?"

He sighed, his green eyes so much like his niece's sad and shadowed, worry tracing new lines into his face. "It's not a good thing that's happened, Faith. The crate back there is done up like a coffin, and it has all of our pictures in it."

"A coffin?" Faith paled, the freckles sprinkled across her nose dark in contrast. "A coffin? With our pictures?" She started to shake. "They really mean it, don't they, Uncle Seth? How do we stay safe?"

"Andrew and Bill are working on a plan. But now, let's go find Stringbean. He's here to see about either expanding this building or putting up a whole new one for us. What would be your preference?"

"New, I think. Can we really do this, Uncle Seth?"

He nodded, his mind tracking back to when she was little and asked him that. A single man raising two young children had been hard, but Faith had challenged him the most. What did a man really know about raising a girl? She'd turned out all right, the good Lord had seen to that, he thought. She deserved to have a new building.

"We can. Now what would you like to see in it? Here's Stringbean. Let's talk to him."

Chapter 10

$\mathcal{A}$ week later, Faith turned from watching Stringbean and his crew work on their new building. They had chosen well, she thought. The building was steel, which is what Stringbean had recommended. She laughed at his name. Yes, she thought, her mother would have described him as a long drink of water. She shivered as she walked towards the store, eyes searching the area. She knew someone was watching them, had been for weeks, just waiting in the shadows before they brought more destruction and damage and please God, not death, to them.

She stopped, staring at the man standing ten feet in front of her, fear coursing through her. He wasn't supposed to be near her. What did Watson want?

"Faith, so nice to see you without anyone else around you."

"Why are you here? You're not to be near me."

He flicked his fingers. "A misunderstanding, my dear. Come, we'll go somewhere and talk it over and come to an understanding." He stretched out a hand.

She backed away from him, searching for someone to help her. "Not a misunderstanding, Ted. You know that quite well. I want you gone." She reached into the pocket of her jacket, pulling out her phone, praying she could hit the right buttons on her phone and that help would reach her before she disappeared. Because disappear she would, she knew. Ted had a dark side not many people saw. She had seen it with other women and knew there would be no reprieve for her, just because she had taken out a restraining order.

He paced slowly towards her, a cruel smile playing around his lips. "No one's going to hear you cry. The men are making too much noise. Your uncle won't be coming to your rescue."

"What did you do to Uncle Seth?"

"Nothing that a little aspirin won't cure." He reached for her arm and pulled her towards him, knocking her phone flying from her hand.

She fought him, her nails raking across his face, leaving bloody furrows in their wake. He backhanded her and she tasted the copper taste of blood in her mouth and her jaw sending shooting pains through her face. She struggled to get away, her jacket sleeve ripping at the strength with which he pulled her towards his car. There was no way she was getting into it.

"Stop fighting me, Faith. You're mine. We belong together."

Faith broke free and ran for the construction site, fear lending speed to her feet. She was tackled to the ground and his weight held her down, her screams echoing through the air.

"Don't try that again, my dear. It won't work, you know? You'll never get away."

"And I say she will." Ted had not heard the footsteps running towards him.

Josiah had heard Faith's screams as he stepped down from his truck and ran in the direction they came from. His heart in his throat, he pulled Ted off and away from Faith.

"Faith, run. Go to the construction crew. Have them call 911." He ducked as a fist was swung at him, then swung his own fist, a satisfying crunch coming from Ted's nose.

Ted crumpled to the ground, curses flying from his mouth. Josiah reached down and drew Ted's belt from his waist, using it to bind his hands behind his back.

Josiah looked up as he heard footsteps running towards him. Stringbean and one of his crew were heading his way, Josiah not sure if it was James or John, a set of twins that was working on the building.

"We need to find Seth. He's around here somewhere."

The crew member nodded and headed for the shop as sirens wailed in the distance, coming closer with each heartbeat Josiah could feel.

"Ted Watson? What'd he do? No, I don't need to ask. I guess the rumours and innuendos we've all heard are true." Stringbean stared down at him, then back towards the building site. "Faith's really shaken up. We'll need to have someone look at her face."

"Her face?" Josiah spun to stare at the other man.

"She said he hit her across the face before he tackled her. We could barely understand her. What is it with you two? Not enough excitement in your lives?"

Josiah shook his head as he gave a half-smile. "Too much excitement, I'm thinking." He looked up as Bill ran his way, followed by three other officers.

"Watson? Faith?"

Josiah nodded. "He tried to kidnap her after assaulting her. She's with the construction crew right now. Stringbean says we need to get someone to look at her face."

Bill's face hardened as he stared down at Watson. "We have him now, do we, Josiah? We can finally lock him away?"

Josiah nodded. "You can. Faith will testify, I know. She's wanted him out of her life for ages now."

Watson struggled as the officers pulled him to his feet and removed his belt to place handcuffs on his wrists.   A sudden movement and he had an officer's gun in his hand, pointed directly at Josiah.

"No, this isn't happening this way. Faith and I are leaving."   The gun shook from the rage coursing through his body.

Bill tried to talk him into handing over the gun, but Watson refused, the gun pointing directly at Josiah. Josiah watched, knowing that if he made a move he would be shot, most likely dead. A movement to the side caught his attention. No, Faith. Not now. A shot rang out, and Watson crumpled to the ground, the gun dropping beside him, his life gone in an instant.

Bill stared at the man and then around. "Who fired that shot?"

The officers spun in a circle, trying to determine just where the shot had come from.

"It wasn't us, Bill. It came from the trees over there."

He nodded as two of the officers ran that way. "I don't think they'll find anyone.

Someone made sure he didn't get away again."

Josiah nodded, half turning as he heard running footsteps, then felt a body slam into him, almost taking him down. Faith clung to him, her face buried in his shirt. Hugging her tight, he looked up at Bill's nod.

"Come on, Faith. Let's get you away from here. Ezra and Sue are here. Let them take a look at you."

She shook her head, not moving from where she stood, arms clinging even tighter. Josiah finally sighed and swung her up in his arms, heading for where the paramedics stood waiting, Seth nearby.

"Is she okay, Josiah?" Seth's voice was laced with worry.

Josiah nodded. "I think so. He roughed her up, and we need to get that looked at. Faith, Honey, come on. Let me set you down on the stretcher. Let us see your face."

Faith refused to lift her head, and Josiah shot a look at Sue. She shook her head.

"Set her on the stretcher, Josiah. Don't let go of her. She needs to know she's safe." Sue reached for Faith's face, gently turning it towards her, cringing when she saw the massive bruise on her cheek and the blood on her mouth. "Faith, can you move your jaw?" She watched as Faith shook her head.

Josiah watched, concern filling his face. "He broke it?" A sound from Seth had him raising his head to look at him.

Ezra spoke. "I would say he did. We need to get her laying down, though, to transport her."

Later that night, Josiah turned from the window in Faith's hospital room, watching as Seth slumped in a chair nearby, half asleep. He had been knocked out by Ted Watson, but other than a headache was fine. Faith mumbled and turned in her sleep, the painkillers given her not quite dulling the pain totally. Thank you, Lord, he thought. At least her jaw isn't broken, but it will take time to heal from the blow.

He headed for the door, needing to pace, and not wanting to disturb either one. Once in the hallway, he walked towards the waiting room, then stopped. No, he needed the chapel, didn't he? He turned, seeing Bill and Andrew walking towards him.

"How's Faith?" Andrew voiced the concern of both men.

"Her jaw's not broken, but it's pretty sore. She'll be a while getting over it." Josiah stared past them, eyes narrowed as he saw the same man again. "There's that guy again, the one that keeps coming into the shop."

Bill turned partway but by that time the man had left. "We pulled a photo from the security feed, but haven't had any luck tracking him down. Andrew thinks we'll need to pull in national databases."

Andrew nodded. "If he's even in one. I have a feeling he won't be." He looked back at the door to Faith's room. "How is Seth?"

"He hurting, Andrew. He wants this over yesterday. It's not just about Watson. It's everything."

Andrew nodded. "It is. We're working on it. Brownlee finally turned over some evidence, but I don't think it's all of it."

Josiah snorted. "It won't be. I have a feeling the son is involved in this somehow." He looked up at the ceiling, his heart raising in prayer for healing and strength. He somehow knew it was far from over.

Chapter 11

Faith turned as she heard steps behind her on the sidewalk. She frowned, not recognizing the man walking towards her. He nodded at her and walked past, heading for the local hardware store. She studied him. Now, why did he seem familiar? It had been a week since Ted Watson had been killed, and they were still working on that. She shook her head. She was glad he was gone, but did it really have to have been the way it was? Her face was still healing and so was her heart.

Josiah stopped behind Faith, watching as she searched the area around her. What will it take to make her feel safe again, Lord? Help me to help her. Faith turned with a smile as she heard him approach her.

"Did you get everything you were after?" he asked as he reached for the bags she was carrying, then grasped her hand in his.

"I think so. We need to stop at the grocery store for some supplies, then I'm done." Her words were still difficult for her to get out, but it was improving. "I'll be glad when I can eat something more than soup and jelly."

He laughed. "Not enjoying it any more, are you? Beth said she was bringing in something special for you today, Faith. She wouldn't say what it was." His eyes searched the area around them, hating the feeling of being watched.

Seth turned as the two approached him, handing him the newspapers he had asked for. "Stringbean says the shell of the building is done and they can start putting up the partitions. He needs us to go through where we want them, Faith. Up to doing that? Beth is hard at work at that new design you've come up with. She says it's one of the best she's ever seen."

Faith snorted. "Yeah, well, go through what I did, and the imagination sparks."

Josiah watched as the two turned to walk away, then surprised, felt Faith's hand catch his, drawing him with her. Puzzled, he studied her face, nodding when she smiled at him. Okay, so now what?

At the end of the day, Beth watched as Faith moved among the displays in the store. She had come to love this young woman as a daughter and knew she was hurting in a way that needed a woman's advice.

"Faith?" Beth had to speak her name more than once to get her attention. "Come, sit with me. It's just us ladies here for now. Talk to me. You're troubled."

Faith sighed as she sank onto one of the stools, finger running along the edge of the work table, eyes on the floor. "I am, Beth. And I just want my Mom." Tears sparkled in her eyes when she looked up.

Beth reached for her and drew her into a hug. "Tell me, Faith. Talk to me like you would your Mom. I can't take her place, but I would like to help you."

Faith poured out what was bothering her, the words mumbled at times at the speed she was talking.

"Faith, what you're feeling is normal. You are under attack, not just from a physical source, but a spiritual one as well. That's why we're told to buckle on our armour every day. You understand that, don't you?" Beth waited until Faith nodded. "Okay. Now, I don't know you well enough to know if you've ever had a boyfriend, but you have someone now who would like to be that. Josiah is interested in you, but is moving slowly as he finds his way back to our Father. He knows you would want him to do that before you even think about a relationship with him."

Faith's eyes traced past Beth, not focusing on what she was seeing. "And he is. This is what scares me, Beth. Uncle Seth did his best, but I didn't have my mother when I needed her."

Beth shook her head. "No, you didn't but you had ladies in your life that stepped up. I know that because Seth told me that. Now, you are going to have to spend time in prayer, my dear. Find out what God wants. He hasn't placed Josiah here just for now. Everyone can see the attraction between you two. It's up to you two to figure out what you want."

Faith nodded. "I know and that scares me, Beth. This isn't something I want to mess up."

Beth laughed. "You won't. You remind me of the woman in Proverbs 31. Study that passage, Faith. You are a picture of it. Josiah knows that well. He'll be wanting to find out where he stands with you one of these days. Pray and be prepared to be honest with him." With that, she dropped a kiss of Faith's head and with a hug, walked out of the building, heading home for the day.

Faith watched as Georgia romped over the floor, finally coming to jump up on her knee. She stroked the silky fur of the kitten as she contemplated Beth's words. She knew in her heart what she wanted, but she didn't know what Josiah did. She sighed, knowing that they couldn't go forward until what they were facing was done.

Josiah stopped in the doorway, fading light reflecting through the opening, framing him. He watched Faith for a few minutes, then silently made his way to the computer, pulling up the website he had designed. His hacker friend hadn't been able to get in, so he was happy. He hadn't heard from the group for a while, which he thought strange.

Speaking of which, he thought, there's an email from them. He opened it, reading through it slowly, then turning to face the lady he had come to love. Yeah, he finally admitted it to himself, he thought.

"Faith, I've heard from the group."

She approached, her hand resting on his shoulder. "What do they have to say?"

"They're pleased with the website and the encrypted email address I set up. They're getting responses, far more than they thought or expected. Whoever it is that's after money is targeting more businesses, working out and away from just the artists."

"Oh, I don't like that." Faith's voice had her concern.

"No, I don't either. I just wish we knew who it was."

"Are there any leads at all?"

Josiah shook his head. "I haven't heard that there are. Bill and Andrew I know are still investigating, but it's not a real priority with them. They have other investigations that need to be done."

She sighed. "That's what I thought you would say." She turned to stare around the work room. "How do we continue to live under this cloud hanging over us? Can't we go on the offensive or something like they do in sports?"

Josiah turned, his eyes on her face. "Now, that's a thought. I wonder how we can."

"Josiah! I didn't really mean that, you know!" Faith was shocked at his response.

"I know you didn't, sweetheart, but it's something to consider." He pulled out his phone. "Let me see if I can round up some of my friends. They can help."

"How?"

Josiah started to laugh. "They have wild imaginations. Zeke is one who really thinks outside the box. We've told him he's chased one too many storms."

"Chased storms?"

"He's a meteorologist and loves to chase bad storms, the wilder the better." He looked up at her, then reached to lay his hand on her cheek with the fading bruise, surprised that she leaned into his hand. "We'll come up with something."

"Have you heard from Noah lately? Neither Uncle Seth or I have." She was worried about her cousin.

"No, I haven't, come to think of it. But when he gets involved in his work, it's not surprising that we don't. I've sometimes gone three weeks without even getting an email from him. He's intense, you know? Just like someone else I know."

She glared at him, then patted his head. "Thanks, I think."

A thud from the back door startled them, and they spun. Josiah was on his feet, moving towards it, when it flew open. The man who had been harassing them entered, looking around the shop

"Still not paying, Faith? My bosses are getting angry. You don't want to make them angry." His finger pointed at her, then at Josiah. "Pretty boy here may have an accident because of you. Or your uncle. Or your cousin. I would hate to see them hurt. Just like someone in your past." He dropped a bag on the table. "I'll be back tomorrow.

Have our money in that bag." He was gone before she could answer.

"What did he mean, Josiah, when he said that about my past? Was Uncle Seth right about the plane crash?'

Josiah wrapped her in a hug. "I think he might have been, Faith. My friend had some information she was sending me later about that. We'll figure it out. Now about that bag."

Seth stood in the store doorway. He had entered just as the door shut behind the man. "We're not paying, Faith. Not a chance. Andrew is on his way out. He says he has some information for us. And for the record, thank you, Josiah, for taking the steps to find out about the crash."

Chapter 12

$\mathcal{F}$aith stared at Andrew as he spoke, unsure of what she was hearing.

"Who did you say you suspect of being the leader of these men?"

"It's not the chief, we've determined that.   Our investigation has led us in a different direction, and I know you would like to hear the name, but this person is prominent part of the community.   That person works in a local office. I don't want to say too much until we have confirmed our information and have made an arrest. We're not to that point yet." He turned to Josiah. "You say the collector was back again."

Josiah nodded. "He dropped off that bag and told us to have it ready with the money tomorrow. Here's what I'd like to do instead."

Josiah spoke quickly, outlining his plans. The three men stared at him and then one another.

"It might work, Josiah, but it's very risky for you and Seth and of course, Faith." Andrew was concerned about their safety.

"We know it is, but we can't continue like we are." Seth paced the room. "Let's go for it, Josiah. Confirm what you need to, then place that information in the bag and leave the bag outside on the walk tomorrow. I'll let Stringbean and his crew know not to come around tomorrow, just for their safety."

Faith spoke, a puzzled frown on her face. "Has anyone asked Stringbean if he's been approached?"

"I have and he hasn't been." Seth looked over at Andrew. "I know you're not totally on board, Andrew, but we have to come up with a plan. Josiah has another couple of plans. One I really don't like, but we'll use it if we have to."

"I hope you let us in on it."

Josiah nodded. "If we have to use it, we will. Let's pray we don't." He pulled out his phone as it chimed. "Good. Three of my friends are free tomorrow and the next day and are willing to help come up with some more plans."

Bill started to laugh. "If it's Zeke, look out world."

Josiah grinned. "It is. I wonder what he'll come up with."

Andrew stared between the two men. "Zeke, as in the storm chaser Zeke?"

"That's him!" Bill laughed harder. "He always has good plans. He must have driven his parents crazy as a youngster."

The next morning, Josiah left the bag on the walk to the store, then grasping Faith's hand, pulled her to his truck and tucked her inside.

"What are you doing, Josiah?" She stared at him as he climbed behind the wheel.

"Getting us out of here. Seth has already left."

"He has? I didn't hear him go. But what about Beth?"

"She knows not to come this morning. Bill will be hanging out here to make sure no damage is done."

"All right, then. So we're in running mode. Where are we running off to?"

Josiah threw her a quick grin, then sobered. "Logan City. I'm meeting Zeke, Darius, and Samuel there, and they wanted to meet you too. We're needing to make some plans, more than what we have already. We're far from done with these guys."

Faith nodded, then sighed. "I must say your friends certainly have uncommon names."

Josiah laughed at that. "We do, don't we?"

Faith sat back on Jonah's couch a couple of hours later, flushed with laughter, Josiah at her side. Zeke, Jonah and Darius had come up with some outrageous plans, and Josiah just seemed to go along with them. She hadn't seen the looks the four men had been exchanging.

Josiah looked down at his phone as it chimed. "The collector's been around and taken the bag. Bill said he tried the doors on the building and then checked out the new one. He was not very happy looking."

Zeke shook his head. "Did you think he would be? Tell us. What did you place in the bag?"

Josiah hesitated, his eyes dropping to Faith, who had tilted her head to look up at him.

"I confirmed his identity with a friend and let documentation on that in the bag. Also a warning that we were coming for them and that we wouldn't pay." He sighed. "It's very risky, I know, but both Faith and Seth are determined to stop this."

Faith nodded. "We do. I've had enough of this living in fear." The men watched as her fingers touched the fading bruise on her face and then three sets of eyes raised to Josiah, before exchanging glances, small smiles on their faces. Josiah had found his lady, they all thought. Now to keep her safe.

"What do you do next, Faith? What if he comes back tomorrow and demands more money?"

Faith shook her head. "It's not happening. We go on with our lives, our hands in our Father's, and then do the best we can. God is there, even in this." Her eyes searched the faces of the men in front of her as they nodded. Josiah's arm wrapped around her and pulled her close.

Josiah spoke. "We have some plans that Seth and I have come up with. Neither one of us will say what they are, but one is pretty daring." He paused, eyes staring into the distance. "You know, when you're a child, you expect the world to be the same when you're an adult. That doesn't happen, and it takes some getting used to."

Seth turned from the window in the store two days later and headed for the work room.

"He's back, people. Let Josiah deal with him. Beth, Faith. In there." He pointed at the room Josiah was using. "Stay there until we tell you to come out." The women shared a frightened look and disappeared as the back door opened.

"Where is he?" The collector was angry.

137

"Who?"

"You know, that young fellow." He started pacing through the shop, looking around. He tried the door where the women were hiding and found it locked. "Open that."

Seth shook his head. "No. The women are in there and I won't let you near them."

The collector approached Seth, fist raised, then halted in his tracks at the voice behind him.

"I think that's enough, sir. You are under arrest for assault, for extortion, and whatever else we can come up with." Bill grasped the man's wrists and slid the handcuffs on them. He nodded at Seth and then shoved the man towards the officers with him. "Take him in, fellows, and book him. He'll lawyer up and be out I would say in a short time. See what you can do to keep him there as long as you can. I know other municipalities are interested in him. And if I am not mistaken, there will be a few murders on the books with his name on them."

Seth watched with Bill as the officers disappeared, then tapped at the door to alert the women they could come out.

"Is it over, Bill?"

Bill shook his head. "No, it's not, Seth. Now that we've arrested one of the men, the others will be coming after you even harder and stronger." He turned to face them, noting Josiah standing behind Faith. "This is where it gets very dangerous. Mom, if you're out, we understand."

Beth snorted, drawing their eyes to her. "Bill, you know better. I have never backed down from a challenge in my life. Even your father wants to be involved." She turned to Seth. "Didn't you say you needed an accountant? That's what Will is. He'll come in a day or two a week to help out. He's a retired officer, injured on the job. He's worked through the years as an accountant on the side as well."

Seth nodded. "That's fine, Beth. We can use him."

Josiah watched as Faith paced away, worry etched on her face. She spun, her eyes on him. "What now, Josiah? What plans do you have for us? I know you and Uncle Seth have been talking."

Josiah walked forward and stopped in front of her, eyes not leaving her face. "We do, Faith.   We have set some in place already. We're not saying much about what they are, and you know why."

She nodded, then spun on her heel and walked away. When, Lord, she asked, when will we be safe once again?

Chapter 13

The loud banging on the house door woke both Seth and Faith in the early morning two days later. Seth stood on the porch, deep in conversation with Josiah and Andrew, as Faith approached, questions on her face.

"Uncle Seth?"

The men turned and she stepped back at the grim look on their faces.

"What is it?"

Seth sighed. "The collector is loose again. Andrew said he was being transported to Riverville and the cruiser was run off the road."

"Oh no! Are the officers safe?"

Andrew nodded. "They are, but the collector's buddies made some pretty heavy threats against the three of you. I'm placing an officer here on site at all times for the next while. Even then, I can't guarantee you'll be safe. Stay together as much as you can. If you need to leave here for anything, let me know and I'll send someone to go with you."

"You can't keep that up forever, Andrew." Faith studied Josiah's face, knowing he was working on another plan. "Have you found out any more information?"

Andrew shook his head. "We're amassing a lot of information and charges against him. We've identified and arrested some of his cohorts, but there are still a number out there. We also don't have enough yet to charge the person in control."

"What about any of the other businesses?" Josiah knew the others had been happy, he had gotten that word over the website.

"I would think they're in fear again. I can't get anyone to talk with me, other than you." Andrew was frustrated.

"Fear will do that." Josiah turned as he heard a vehicle coming towards them and squinted through the brightening sky. "Now what is Zeke doing here at this time of the morning?"

Zeke ran for the porch, envelope in hand. "Josiah, Andrew. Just the two I wanted to see. Your friend came through again, Josiah. Here's the information her company found. Gotta run. There's a beautiful storm brewing to the west." He was gone before they could say anything to him.

Josiah stared at the envelope in his hand, knowing the questions he had asked and knowing that once he opened the envelope, there would be no going back.

"Josiah?" Faith's quiet voice roused him from his reverie and her soft hand on his own hand had him raising his head to look at her.

"This is going to blow everything apart, if the answers are what I think they are." He turned and walked down the steps, away from them, their eyes following him.

Josiah sat slumped on the bench near the front of the store, staring at the papers in his hands. It was much worse than he thought. Feeling a hand on his shoulder, he looked up. Faith stood there, concern on her face, a puzzled look in her eyes. She noted the bleakness of his expression, wondering what had caused it.

"Josiah?"

He took her hand and pulled her down beside him, then wrapped an arm around her, pulling her close. She watched as he bit at his lips, trying to find the words he needed.

"What is it, Josiah? Is it really that bad?"

He nodded, not looking at her. "It is, Faith. It really is. He stared ahead of him. "It's what I expected or even more than that. It's about your parents' accident." He hesitated. "Faith, this is where your trust in God will have to hold you up and steady you. I'm trying to work that out for myself with Him."

She had a hand on his arm. "I know you are and I see it happening." She stood, pulling him upright with him. "Come, let's go talk with Seth and Andrew. They're waiting in the house for us." She watched as the construction crew pulled in and headed for the building. She knew she and Seth would need to head over there soon, but this needed to be addressed first.

Seth looked up as Josiah followed Faith into the kitchen, then pointed at the table. "Sit. We'll have something to eat before we delve into what you've found, Josiah."

Pushing aside his plate, Josiah reached for the envelope, hesitant to bring what he had found out into the open. At the silence around him, he looked up, finding their eyes on him. He looked at Seth, who nodded.

"Father, what we have here only You know how it will affect all of us and what it means to what is now going on. Grant us the wisdom, peace, and strength that we need." Heads stayed bowed after Seth finished, then raised.

Josiah sighed, then pulled out three copies of what he had been given. He handed on to Seth, one to Andrew, then looked at Faith, who moved her chair over closer to him.

"Let me preface this by saying my friend did most of the research as well as one of her employees. She did pull in an investigator for part of it, but I know him as well and he is completely thorough and trusty." Josiah's eyes were focused on the papers. "I didn't realize I would find out the truth after so many years. Read through what you have and then we'll talk about it."

Andrew read through his copy, then pulling out his pen, read back through, marking passages and making notes. He finally glanced up at Josiah, noting the strain and stress putting fresh lines on the younger man's face. Well, not that much younger, Andrew thought. He had made lieutenant at a young age, younger than most he knew.

Seth finally sat back, watching his niece, knowing how this would affect her. He could see the tears she was fighting to hide.

"Faith?"

Seth's quiet voice was her undoing. She buried her head on her arms and sobs wracked her body. Josiah's hand rubbed up and down her back. Andrew and Seth shared a glance, then both looked back at their paperwork.

"All these years, Andrew. It's been there and buried all these years. It took this young fellow the courage to go where we didn't."

"I know, Seth. I think we just buried our heads in the sand." Andrew sighed. "You'll be having to call Noah, won't you?"

Seth nodded, then glanced as Josiah moved. "What did you do, Josiah?"

"I had my friend send a copy of this to Noah. I don't know when he'll get it, but he will have a copy as well." He paused, then looked down. "I think I overstepped my bounds."

Faith looked up at him, her face drenched with her tears. "No, Josiah. You didn't. You did what we would do. Thank you."

Josiah nodded, then watched as Andrew shared a look with Seth. "What did you find, Andrew?"

Andrew stared into the distance, then sat back in his chair. "She's good, your friend. She found information that had been hidden during the initial investigation. It wasn't an accident after all, was it? She clearly implicates Brownlee, his brother, and two of their friends."

Seth nodded. "We've always questioned those four. I guess we know now how Brownlee got to be chief."

"What do you mean, Uncle Seth?" Faith was puzzled at his words.

"His two friends were on the town council at the time he was put in as chief."

Josiah stared down at his papers, then back up. "The council is corrupt as well?"

Seth shook his head. "No, that's not what I'm saying. Brownlee used to be able to hide very well, but he's gotten careless. Andrew, you say he came back clean? How is that possible, given this?"

Andrew nodded. "I'm pulling someone else in to do the investigation again. I've talked to the head detective in Oak City. He's a good friend and will do the investigation on the quiet for me. I'll need to get him this information as well." He sat back and sighed. "It just doesn't end, does it?"

Standing near his truck a few days later on his way to a meeting, Josiah turned as he heard heavy footsteps behind him and was on the ground, head spinning from the savage blow before he could completely turn. The pain from the kick to the ribs had him doubling up. He vaguely heard voices talking to him and then blackness.

Seth saw the men coming towards the house and pushed Faith out the back door, grabbing her hand and running for a hillock at the back. He yanked open the door, sending her down the few stairs and following her, locking the door behind them and dropping a large metal bar across the doorway. Please, Lord, let Josiah be safe. Keep us in the hollow of Your hand. He pulled out his phone, sending a quiet call to 911 and then to Andrew.

What seemed hours later to Faith found Andrew calling for Seth from the back yard. Seth unbarred the doors and opened them, cautiously leaving the shelter. Andrew walked towards them.

"What happened, Seth? Stringbean and his crew didn't hear anything."

Seth nodded, not surprised. "I saw the collector and two other men headed towards the house and just grabbed Faith and ran." He looked around. "I take it they're gone?"

"They are.   They didn't do any damage in your house, other than kicking in the front door. The shop's the same."

"Where's Josiah?"   Faith's quiet question had the men turning to her.

"He's not with you?" Andrew started to turn."

"No, he's not. He had headed for his truck. He said he had a meeting in Logan City."

"Do you know who with?"

Seth shook his head. "Did he tell you, Faith?"

"No. I thought maybe it was with a client from the way he spoke, but I can't be sure." She turned as she heard a phone ringing. "That's strange. Where's that phone?"

They searched, Andrew finally tracking down the ringing. Picking it up, he answered it, surprise lining his face as he talked. Thoughtfully he stared at it when the conversation finished.

"Andrew?" Bill had come up to him as he finished.

"This is Josiah's phone. He never made it to his meeting."

"That explains why his truck is still here, but where is he?"

"Fan out and search. He's got to be here somewhere. Faith, you and Seth head for your shop. I want you two inside."

Faith looked up from her work, eyes hopeful when Andrew and Bill entered the work shop a couple of hours later, her heart falling at the looks on their faces.

"No sign of him, Faith and Seth. He's disappeared." Andrew looked down at the evidence bags he was holding. "We have his wallet, his keys, his phone, and his portfolio. Just not him."

Faith looked devastated and Beth wrapped an arm around her, watching Andrew closely.

"So where is he then, Andrew?" Seth asked the question they all wanted an answer to.

"We don't know. He's not around here anywhere, not that we can see." Andrew's eyes tracked between Seth and Faith. "It looks as if whoever was here with the collector took him with them. He will no doubt be used to try and get you to cooperate and pay the money they're asking. And I can guarantee the amount will have risen substantially."

Seth nodded. "That's my thinking." He sighed. "We got him involved through no fault of his own. Now we have to find him. But how?"

"Did you get a look at any vehicles today, Seth?"

"No, just the men. Did the cameras pick up anything?"

Bill shook his head. "No, they kept far enough back that they weren't real clear. I've taken a copy of the section we need and hope one of our techs can clean it up enough to at least get a description."

Chapter 14

Josiah stirred, his eyes cracking open slightly, the light sending a piercing pain through his head. He reached for his head, but his hands refused to move. He tried once again to reach for the pain in his chest, but his hands still wouldn't move. He tried to roll over but the swirling darkness claimed him once more. He didn't feel the bumps in the road that sent his head rolling and banging on the window he was leaning against.

The men with him watched him, then turned back to their conversation. What did they do with him now?   The collector wanted to take him to their boss, to hold him to make Faith pay, but the other two men wanted to get rid of him right then and there. Arguments broke out, and momentary inattention to the rocky road lead to disaster, the car drifting to the side of the road and then down into a deep ditch and plowing through saplings and underbrush, the vehicle finally crumpling against a larger tree, hidden from the road. The four men lay still, dust swirling into the air from the accident, leaves and other debris sifting down onto the vehicle.

Josiah stirred once more, fumbling for his seat belt and tumbling out the door he was able to force open. On hands and knees, he tried to get his bearings, finally raising his head to look around. He stumbled to his feet, not knowing where he was, his head swinging as he searched the area for something familiar. He dropped back to his knees, his hands cradling his head. How long he remained like that, he didn't know, but he finally struggled back upright again, and forced his way through the underbrush. He felt the rain starting, the drops finding their way through the leafy canopy above him.

The old man reined his horse to a halt, studying the ground in front of him. He dismounted, leaving the reins dropping to the ground, and made his way towards the vehicle. He reached inside and turned off the ignition out of habit even though he couldn't hear the motor running, then reached to feel for pulses. They were still alive, the three men, but he knew they needed help soon. He moved back to his horse and then past it up to the road, his cell phone out, his hand hovering for a moment over the keypad before he dialled for help, thankful that for once he had enough of a signal to do so.

The emergency personnel mingled around the road, lane really, and searched for clues. The men in the car had been removed and transported to hospital, under guard.

Andrew approached the patrol officer in charge, pulling out his badge. The men had crossed into a new county during the drive into the forest.

"Andrew. How are you?" Sergeant Tad Barrett moved to shake his hand. "What brings you here?" He paused, then pointed behind him. "Those men are the ones you were looking for?"

Andrew nodded, his gaze going back behind him to where Faith and Seth stood. "They were. We think they kidnapped a friend of those two standing there. It's a long story but the brief version is that there's a protection racket running and those two have been targeted, and their friend was helping them fight back."

Tad turned to watch Faith and Seth. "Her boyfriend?"

Andrew shrugged. "It's looking that way. Now, where is he? There were only the three in there when you found them?"

Tad nodded. "From what Old Wiley said, it looks as if the accident happened sometime yesterday. With the rain we've had, it's hard to tell if someone else was there. Although…". Tad stopped speaking, turning to search. "There's Old Wiley. He's a fixture up here in the forest. If anyone could find their friend, it would be him. He did say the one back door was open when he got there."

"And you're saying that tracking dogs not likely would be of help."

Tad shrugged. "It's possible, depending on what way your friend went and if the rain didn't wash away the scent. That would be my concern."

Tad looked past Andrew as he sensed movement, causing Andrew to turn.

"Faith?"

"Was he here, Andrew? Is Josiah safe?" Her eyes pleaded with him to say yes.

"We don't know yet, Faith. There's some evidence suggesting a fourth person was here, but we don't know for sure if it was Josiah." He reached a hand to keep her from falling as she staggered. "We were just trying to determine if we could bring in search dogs."

"And what did you decide?" She looked between the two officers.

Tad shook his head. "I'm not sure if it would work, given the rain we've had for the last twelve hours."

"Can we try?" Faith felt like she was begging, but she just needed to find Josiah.

Tad stared at her for a moment before looking away and studying the terrain. Finally, he nodded. "I have a team on the way in, but we'll need something of your friend's."

Faith handed him the bag she had been holding. "Here. This is a T-shirt I know he wore three days ago and was in his laundry."

Tad looked at it and then up at her. "How did you know to bring something?"

She shrugged. "I asked God what I should do, and He said this."

Tadd stared at her, then at Andrew, who shrugged. Tad shook his head as he moved off towards an arriving vehicle, one he knew would hold the search team.

"What are the chances, Andrew?" Faith's eyes watched Tad as he walked away.

"I won't lie to you, Faith. They're not good, not with the rain we've had."

She nodded. "That's what I thought you would say." She sighed and leaned her head against her uncle's shoulder. "Uncle Seth, why?"

"The good Lord knows, Child. We need to leave it with him. Come, sit back in the car. It's going to be a long day."

Six hours later, Tad approached Andrew. "No luck, Andrew. They tracked him for a while, then lost him at a stream. It was a pretty open area so the rain may have well washed away his tracks."

Andrew nodded, not wanting to face Seth and Faith. "Any chance we can spread out and search further?"

"I'll put you in touch with a civilian search and rescue team, but it's too late in the day now for them to start. Take those two home and call me later." He handed over his card. "My cell's on there, although I'll likely still be at the office."

Andrew took the card, turning it over and over in his hand. "I hate this part of the job, Tad, knowing someone's out there and not being able to find them."

Tad nodded. "I know. The thing is we don't know if he was hurt before the accident or in the accident or even if he's still alive out there."

Andrew nodded once again, a somber look on his face. "I hear you. I have to call his parents and that's not a call I want to make. Faith is taking it hard."

"What the situation between those two?"

Andrew shrugged. "I'm not really sure. I know they were spending a lot of time together, but that could have been Josiah protecting her as much as he could."

Faith watched as Andrew and Tad walked towards her, her heart falling. Tears gathered in her eyes and she felt her uncle's arm around her.

"I'm sorry, Faith. Seth. The dog tracked him for a while, but lost his scent in an open area, likely from the heavy rain last night."

"So, now what. Andrew? Do we just leave and not search any more?" Seth searched the faces of the men in front of him, trying to read what they were thinking.

Tad shook his head. "No. I've given Andrew the name of a civilian search and rescue team. They'll start in the morning." He glanced up at the darkening sky and grimaced. It had been a long day, and he knew they were all exhausted.

"What about the man who found the vehicle?" Faith searched for him.

Tad shook his head. "He's moved out once we had the situation in our hands. He's a hard person to keep track of, he's too used to being on his own."

"Please, can we try?"   Faith was grasping for anything that might find Josiah.

Tad looked at her, then nodded. "It's too late in the day to find his place, but I'll send someone up tomorrow. Just understand that Old Wiley roams these woods all the time and may not be at home."

She nodded. "Please, just try. That's all I ask."   She turned towards Seth as he touched her shoulder.

"Come, Faith.   Andrew's waiting to take us home. They'll keep us updated."

Chapter 15

Seth watched as a younger man entered their shop, looking around. He frowned, then the frown smoothed out. It was Angus Wright, a fellow artist who did pen and pencil sketchings.

"Angus. Welcome. What can I do for you?" Seth reached out to shake his hand.

"Seth. Good morning. It's been a while since I've been here. I've been remiss. Is this Faith's work?"

Seth nodded. "Her designs. We've had to hire someone to help with the work." He turned as he heard Faith behind him. "Faith. Look who dropped in today."

"Faith. Hi. Your work is beautiful." Angus studied the woman about his own age and saw the devastation in her face. They were right, he thought. There's more to Josiah and Faith's relationship than just friendship.

"Thank you, Angus. But that's not why you're here, is it?"

He shook his head as he smiled at her. "No, it's not. I saw your new website and really like it. I was hoping to be able to speak with the designer." He frowned as he caught the look between Faith and Seth. "Faith, is something wrong?"

She nodded, then pointed to the door. "Let's go out and sit in the sun. It's too nice to be inside today."

Once they were settled, she drew a breath. "Have you had any issues with having money demanded from you for payment of protection?"

He shot her a quick glance, then nodded. "I have and I've refused to pay. They're getting more and more demanding. What has that to do with your web designer?"

"Josiah Silverthorn. He's the web designer and has become a good friend. He was helping us trying to find out who was behind it all. He's also found out about my parents' plane crash. The thing is, he's disappeared, almost a week ago, and we can't find him. He was abducted from here."

Angus watched her face. "No sign of him at all?"

She shook her head. "Andrew from the county force has been trying to reach a man called Old Wiley, but hasn't been able to yet. He's the one who found the car the three men were in. One was the collector as we called him."

She suddenly turned to Angus. "You were there that night, Angus. You tried hard to disguise yourself, but I think I recognized you."

Angus stared ahead, not denying, not confirming her words. "There's a group of business owners who are trying to bring this man down. It goes a lot deeper and farther than just collection money, Faith. There's a whole lot more involved, unfortunately. If you knew who the group was, then you would be at far greater risk that you are now."

She nodded. "I understand totally, Angus." She sighed, looking around. "I miss Josiah, you know. I haven't known him for all that long, but he's become a big part of our lives here."

"I'm sure he has. You need to watch yourself, Faith. The group is coming after you soon in a harder and deeper way. The business owners are working to stop all of them, but it's hard. They become so hidden and insidious in their dealings that not many people want to speak up." He paused. "I know Josiah had set up a website and email. Monitor it if you can. Call me if you hear anything?"

Faith nodded as she watched him rise and walk away from her. Where is Josiah, Lord? Is he even still alive? Protect him, please. He has a piece of my heart I've given to no one else and never will.

Faith finally rose and walked back to the shop, her uncle standing outside waiting for her. He was puzzled but reached to hug her.

"What did Angus really want?" He pulled back to study her face.

She sighed. "It wasn't just to find out who our web designer was. I'm sure he was one of the men who talked to Josiah and me that night. Not the one doing the talking or the one behind us." She frowned, walking back through that night in her thoughts. "There was something about the one who seemed to be in charge, who stood behind us. Just a sense that I know him."

"If he's a business owner like you think, you would."

She shook her head. "No, it's more than that. It's like he's been a part of our lives forever."

Seth nodded. "Somehow, Faith, we'll get it all figured." Arm around her shoulder, he turned her to enter the shop. "Beth has some questions that she needs to ask you. And you need to start working on that new design. Josiah would want you to, even though Andrew and Tad haven't been able to find any clue as to where he is."

He turned to look behind him at the sound of vehicle wheels crunching on the gravel driveway. He didn't know the vehicle and his arm tightened around his niece.

The man who exited the vehicle hesitated, looking around, before he headed for them.

"Can we help you?" Seth's voice was cordial, but his green eyes missed nothing, taking in the man's height, graying blond hair and casual clothes.

"I hope you can. Are you Seth Lockwood?"

"I am and this is my niece, Faith. And I would be asking who you are."

"I'm sorry, I should have introduced myself. I'm Josiah's father, Silas. I was sent to find you by the police in Logan City."

"Josiah's father." Faith walked towards him and took his hands. "I'm glad to meet you, but I wish it was under different circumstances."

Silas stared down at the young woman looking up at him and thought, you were right, Julia, you were right. Josiah's voice was different when he talked about this young lady and hers when she talks about him.

"I do too. Have you heard anything at all?"

She shook her head, then turned to the shop, her arm through his as she drew him with her. "No, we haven't. Come in, let us talk it over."

Old Wiley had watched, all those days ago, as the search and rescue teams scoured the area where the first dog had lost Josiah's scent. He had stayed hidden from view, his keen eyes searching the area around. Now, where did you get yourself to, young man? I know you're hurt and you can't have gotten that far. So, where did you hide yourself? He turned, his eyes searching the dense brush through which he knew Josiah had made his way, and then turned back to the stream. You made it this far, but then where did you go? Lord, it's time You clued me in as to where I'm to find him. So far, no one has. I'd like to find him safe and sound for that little girl, Lord, if it be Your will.

He turned back to where he had ground tethered his horse and mounted, his eyes searching as he rode forward. He paused, forearms resting on the saddle horn as he stared around, catching the faint barks of the search dogs wafting towards him on the breeze. He kneed his horse forward, then reined him to a stop as the ears went forward.

"What did you see, boy? What's up there that you think I need to go take a look at?"

Dismounting he moved forward, eyes searching, ears listening. Then he stopped, staring at the ground in front of him before he dropped to his knees. He reached out a hand and found a pulse. He had found Josiah, but now what? He looked around. The search and rescue team were too far away. It would be just him and Roadie to get the young man to shelter and then to safety.

He rose and went to bring Roadie over. The horse bent its head to sniff at Josiah, then stood as Old Wiley struggled to lift the limp body upright and then up onto Roadie's back. He paused when he was finished, his breath coming in gasps. I'm too old for this, Lord. You'll have to give me the strength I need when I get back home.

He swung up behind Josiah, reins in hand and steadied him as he kicked to get Roadie moving forward. It was a heavy load he was asking the aging horse to carry but he wasn't really that far from home. There had been no movement from Josiah, just the faint fall and rise of his back to let Old Wiley know he was still breathing.

Old Wiley dropped the younger man onto his bunk and stood back, arm braced against the wall as he struggled to get his breath back, his heart pounding from the effort. He looked around his cabin, searching for what he needed. Water, he thought, lots of hot water. His medical supplies. He turned to look down at Josiah, noting the torn clothing and the cuts, scrapes and bruising.

He finally stood back, having dressed the wounds that needed it. He had gotten some water down Josiah finally. He pulled the rough woolen blanket up on him and then stepped back, gathering up his pan of water and cloths. He stirred up the fire again and added wood, pulling the kettle forward and then reaching for a pot and meat. He needed to make some broth; he knew the younger man would not be able to get much more than that down him.

He stopped as he left the cabin, heading for the stable, his eyes searching the area. There were only the sounds of the birds and insects and a strengthening breeze stirring the trees, a mixture of evergreen and deciduous. He sighed, wondering how he would care for Josiah. He had no cell phone signal right now, not surprisingly, and he couldn't leave him to go somewhere he would get one. He very seldom had company, which he liked, but today he could use someone stopping by.

A week later, Josiah stirred, his eyes cracking open against the low light from the fireplaces and the lamps. He searched the room, not knowing where he was. His hand felt his head, finding the sore spot and the small bandage now on it. His head turned as he heard soft footsteps and he stared up at the man standing over him, a puzzled look on his face as he tried to place him.

Old Wiley pulled up his chair and sat, reaching to feel for a fever. Josiah's forehead was finally cool. Old Wiley had fought the fever to get it down and save Josiah's life.

"How are you feeling, young man?" Old Wiley's voice was soft, but gruff from disuse.

Josiah wet his lips and tried to speak, nodding when a glass appeared in the old man's hand and his head was raised enough that he could drink. He swallowed, savouring the taste of the lukewarm water. He nodded again, his head laying back on the pillow, his eyes closing as he sank back into sleep.

Old Wiley watched for a while, then rose, setting the chair back at the head of the bunk. He felt old, that night, old and tired. He had fought for a week to keep the younger man alive, tending to his wounds, getting water and broth down his throat as he could. He nodded. Now, tonight he would sleep.

Twelve hours later, Josiah once more stirred, his head clearer and his eyes staying open. He pushed himself higher in the bed, resting his head again the wall behind the pillow, his eyes searching the rough room. Where am I, he thought? Then, it hit him. He had no idea who he was or where he was supposed to be. He could feel the panic starting to rise in him and his eyes slid closed. Soft footsteps once more stopped by his bed and he felt a cool rough hand on his forehead.

"You're awake again, young man. Good. Here, I have some broth for you. I'll help you."

Josiah's eyes opened and he took in the weathered face, brown from the sun and exposure, the rough gray beard and neat but long gray hair. He drew his eyebrows together as he puzzled out who it could be.

Old Wiley smiled, then pulled his chair over to sit by the bunk, holding out the mug of broth. "Just take it easy, young fellow. You've not eaten in at least a week, other than what I could get down you. You'll be drinking this and then sleeping again, I suspect. Any headache or other pain?"

Josiah shook his head, too weak to speak, and drank from the mug, his hand steadied by the older man. Unable to stay awake, his eyes slid shut again.

Old Wiley nodded. He'll be sleeping off and on again for a while, I suspect, won't he, Lord? But that doesn't help me to get him back where he should be. About now would be a good time for You to send someone to visit.

He stood outside in the dusk, staring up at the stars twinkling against the midnight sky, knowing that the clouds were moving in with more rain. He sighed, turning back to stare at his home. There was no way he could leave Josiah long enough to go get help. His family had to be worried about him. He stopped, thinking about the young woman he had seen talking to Tad. His wife? Girlfriend? He could tell from the distance that she wouldn't give up the search.

He turned once again, reaching inside for his rifle as he heard sounds of approaching horses. He moved back to where he was hidden, watching in silence as the two riders stopped, then dismounted.

"Wiley, you around?" It was a woman's voice.

Old Wiley moved forward until he was out in the open.

"It's late for you to be paying a visit, Suzie."

Suzie spun, surprised to see him behind her. "There you are. Something told me to come up to see you tonight, or rather Someone did."

He nodded, then his eyes turned to her companion. "Tad. Surprised to see you here."

"Suzie was adamant she had to come up here and I wasn't about to let her come on her own."

"Let's get your horses settled and then we'll talk. Did you ever find that young man you were searching for?" He nodded as Tad replied in the negative.

The horses settled in the stable, Old Wiley turned to the couple. "Suzie, Tad. That young man you were looking for? I have him in my cabin. He's been pretty sick. I couldn't leave him to go for help, and cell coverage up here has been non-existent."

Tad stopped walking, his eyes on the cabin. "When did you find him?"

"The next day. Your search team headed the wrong way, Suzie."

She nodded. "I'm just glad he's alive. How badly was he hurt?"

"Enough that he can't remember his name or where he lives. I've asked him different times he's roused and all I get is a blank look."

"The men who had taken him hostage lived. They're under guard yet in the hospital, but I'm sure someone from that group is looking for him. We need to get him back to town, but keep it quiet at the same time." Tad's brain was working overtime on this, even as he followed Old Wiley and Susie to the cabin.

Tad stopped as he entered the cabin, his eyes searching for Josiah. Finding him, he walked towards the bunk, noting the fading scrapes and bruises. Josiah was asleep, his face turned towards the wall.

"Has he been awake for any length of time, Wiley?" Tad turned to Old Wiley.

"Not for any great length. Usually just enough to get some liquid down him."

Chapter 16

Tad watched as Suzie and her father talked quietly while seated at the kitchen table. He had chosen a chair where he could watch Josiah, looking for any signs he was awakening.

"Tad, how do you want to do this?" Suzie's voice reached him.

"Do what? Get Josiah back down the mountain?" He rolled his head on the back of the chair to look at his wife.

She nodded. "I don't think he's going to be able to travel for a while yet. Not from what Dad says. If we could get him to the meadow, we could bring in a life flight chopper in. Providing the weather cooperates."

Tad nodded. "We could do that, but that would mean involving more people than we want to. Let me head out in the morning and try to reach Andrew and see what he wants to do."

Suzie rose and walked over to stare down at Josiah as he moaned and tossed his head. "Can we get some painkillers into him, Dad?"

"I haven't been giving him any, Suzie, not knowing his medical history. So far, he's been okay."

She nodded, then reached to feel his face. "He feels a little warm again, Dad. What have you been doing?"

"If Tad can help, we'll get some more water and broth into him. That's been helping, that and cool cloths on the head."

Andrew paused at the door to the work room, his eyes on Faith, then raising to Seth. He had news about Josiah, but he wasn't sure how it would go over. His eyes raised further to study the other man standing there, leaning back against a counter, hands in his pockets. That would be Josiah's father, Andrew thought. Josiah really looks like him. Lord, how do I do this? How do I tell them Josiah is alive, that we can't bring him home yet, and that he has no idea who he is? I know two of these people will want to head right up that mountain, and I can't let them.

"Andrew?" Seth's voice broke into his prayer. "Do you have news?"

Andrew sighed to himself, then nodded. "I do, Seth. That I do." He watched as all of them turned to him.

Silas pushed away from the counter. "Is my son alive?"

Andrew met Silas' eyes. "He is, Mr. Silverthorn. He's been hurt. Someone found him up in the forest and has been caring for him. Because there are no cell phone signals up there, he couldn't call for help. Tad was up there last night and came back down to talk to me."

Faith sat back, relief on her face. "We can bring him back here? And when?"

Andrew dropped his head, his hand rubbing the back of his neck. "That's a problem, Faith. We can't bring him down the mountain for now. He's not strong enough to make the trip. And before you ask, we're not doing a life flight for him.

We need to keep it as quiet as we can that he's still alive. Old Wiley's daughter is a physician and she's checked him out. Tad says he's still sleeping a lot but Suzie doesn't think there's much different that she could do for him even if he was in hospital, other than prescribe rest and as much liquid as they can get down him for now. She's staying now with her Dad."

"I want to go to him, Lieutenant." Silas had walked closer to Andrew.

"I get that, Mr. Silverthorn, but we don't want any of you heading up the mountains where you've never been before. I can guarantee you're being watched right now and they would follow you. From what we've been told, the whole purpose in abducting Josiah was to bring Faith to terms."

"I want to see my son, Lieutenant."

"I understand but you need to understand that Josiah is not safe at this point. Sure, we have the three in custody, but there are more out there." He turned to Faith. "Someone else has been here, haven't they?"

She shared a look with her uncle, then sighed, rising to go over to the desk, reaching into a drawer to withdraw an envelope. "They have been, just yesterday. This is what they left for us."

"And just when were you planning on tell me, Faith? Seth?" Andrew had to tamp down his anger. "You've put yourselves at risk again."

Andrew took the envelope, watching the look on Faith's face, trying to read her thoughts. He opened the letter attached and horror rose in him.

"They've changed what they're asking for? He wants you?"

Faith nodded, her eyes not leaving his face. "They think with Josiah out of the way and my not knowing where he is, whether they have him or not, that I'll jump at the chance to make sure he lives." She turned tortured eyes to Silas. "I'm sorry. Josiah and I were trying to think of a way to tell you and your family and Uncle Seth, but we just couldn't come up with a way." She pulled the necklace she was wearing out from under her shirt and fingered the plain gold band strung on it.

Seth groaned softly, then went to hug his niece. "You two went and got married, didn't you?" He felt her nod against him. "When?"

"The day we met with his friends. We wanted to tell you all, but we never got a chance." She raised her eyes to Silas. "I'm sorry."

He reached out to lay a hand on her head. "Don't be, Faith. I know my son, and he was trying to protect the one he loved and her family. Put that ring back on your finger where Josiah placed it. There's no need to hide the fact any more." He turned to Andrew. "Now, what do we do?"

Andrew shook his head. "I have no idea. What with Faith's news and this threat, I'm really at a loss. I'll need to talk to Tad as well." He spun on his heel and strode away, stopping to fling back over his shoulder. "No more surprises, Faith. It could mean your life or someone else's life if there are."

She sank back down onto her stool and then jumped as Beth laid a hand on hers. "Now, what do we do, Faith? How do we protect you?"

She shrugged. "I don't know, Beth. This scares me. I want to go to Josiah, but I can't. Andrew didn't tell us everything, now did he?" She was up and out of the room before they could stop her, looking for Andrew.

Andrew stood by his car, staring into the distance, trying to wrap his mind around what had just happened. Why, Lord? Why didn't they just tell us? I get that they felt they couldn't, but they should have. This changes it all, now, Lord. How do we go forward? I feel like that broken glass Seth described, shattered into pieces. None of us will ever be the same again, now will we? He turned as he heard footsteps approaching him.

"Andrew?" Faith was hesitant to approach him.

"Faith. Now what are we going to do with you and that threat?"

She shrugged. "I guess we tell them I'm married?"

"And if we do, and they find out to who, his life will be forfeit. You know that, don't you?"

She nodded. "I do." Tears filled her eyes. "Please, Andrew. What else didn't you tell us about Josiah?"

Andrew stared past her, trying to find the words to tell this young bride that her husband didn't even know who he was, let alone know who she was. Lord, I could really use some help here.

"Andrew?"

He looked down at her, then touched her shoulder. "Tad said Josiah was hurt, cuts, scrapes, bruises. He ran a high fever that Old Wiley was able to treat. But.." His voice died away.

"But?"

"He has no memory of who he is, not right now anyway, Faith. Old Wiley has asked him and Josiah can't tell him." He watched with compassion as the tears flowed from her eyes and she angrily swiped them away. "His daughter is with him and she's helping to treat him. But we can't move him just now. It's not a matter of bringing in a vehicle and transporting him out. The only way to get up to Old Wiley's is to walk or by horseback."

Faith nodded. "I understand. I want to go up there, Andrew. Please."

Andrew shook his head. "No, Faith. Not now. They're watching you, monitoring every move you make, just waiting for an opportunity to either nab you or make you pay for what you've put them through. It's become more than just money now. They're after you as a person because you have stood up to them."

"I get that, Andrew. I just want to see Josiah."

"I know you do, Faith. So does his father. But I can't take either of you to him and I have no idea when he'll be able to come down. It will likely be at least a week."

Faith nodded, then shuddered as she searched the area around her. "They're here somewhere, Andrew. What do I do?"

"Let me work on that, Faith. Stay close to someone. Bill's heading out here shortly as well as a couple of other officers. They'll be staying here around the clock for the next while. Now head back in while I can watch you. And lock the doors. Put out the closed sign."

Andrew watched as Faith ran back to the store, then pulling out his phone, sighed.

"Tad? Andrew. We have a new twist in the situation. Apparently Josiah and Faith are married." He held his phone away from his ear at Tad's response. "Yeah! That's what I said. They hadn't told anyone yet." He listened, then spoke. "I agree. It really changes things now. She's adamant she wants to be with him. His father is here as well. Not only that, she's handed me a new threat from the group. The leader no longer wants money. He wants Faith. Yeah, I know. How do we keep her safe? That's my thought. Somehow we'll need to get her away from here. I agree. We need to get those two together somehow."

Andrew spun in a circle, studying the area around him. He could feel the eyes watching him, but could see nothing. "Sure. Let me know what you work out. Right now, she's locked in the shop and Bill and two other officers are on their way out here. My concern is that Seth and Faith won't close their shop for now and they need to."

Andrew turned as two vehicles pulled up beside him and Bill and the other two officers exited them.

"Andrew, what do we have? You're not looking very happy." Bill's voice was quiet, a question on his face.

"I'm not, to tell you the truth, Bill. Tom. April. Glad you two are here. This is what's come up." Andrew walked through what he had just learned.

"Josiah and Faith? Really? No one knew." Bill frowned. "Who married them?"

"I didn't ask. Not that it matters. Tad says we can't get Old Wiley down from the forest yet."

"Well, that certainly puts a new wrinkle on it, doesn't it? What do you want us to do?"

"For now, stay with them. You'll be working around the clock, so work out your schedule. Bill, I think it best if your Mom doesn't come back."

Bill snorted. "That's not happening, Andrew. And I know my Dad will be on his way out here." He turned to scan the area around him. "They're locked in the shop right now, aren't they?"

"They are. Anything at all comes up, contact me. I don't need to tell you three how critical it is to keep them together and safe."

Bill nodded. "I know. There are officers who have volunteered to do the mail run for us. That's a big worry taken away."

Andrew nodded, his glance going to Bill before it turned back to the shop. "I'll be in touch, Bill. Just remember. Nothing goes past you three. No talking about what we've discussed. It's a matter of life and death."

The three nodded. Bill had handpicked the two officers to work with him. But still, something worried at the back of his mind, and he couldn't bring it forward. Lord, I have no idea what it is that bugging me. Bring it to remembrance, please.

Chapter 17

Suzie watched as Josiah's head moved on the pillow and his eyes flickered open. She accepted the mug her father handed her and pulled over a chair to sit by the bunk. Her hand felt Josiah's face. Good, she thought, it's finally cool again.

Josiah turned his head from the light he could see behind his eyelids. Everything hurt, but not as much as before. He opened his eyes, blinking to clear them, then staring around the room. Where was he? What did he last remember? His mind was foggy and he wasn't even sure who he was anymore. Movement caught his attention, and he stared at the woman sitting beside him, mug in hand.

"Good morning, Josiah. You're awake. Here, do you want some water?"

He nodded, tried to rise, and realized he was too weak to prop himself up. The mug was set down and the woman helped him pull himself up, tucking pillows behind him. She handed him the mug, then kept her hand on it as he drank, pulling it back after he had had some, earning herself a glare, at which she grinned.

"How are you feeling today?"

He shook his head, clearing his throat to try and speak. His voice was rusty and hoarse. "Sore. Where am I?"

"You're in my Dad's cabin in the forest. My name's Suzie and I'm a physician. Dad goes by Old Wiley."

"What happened to me?"

"Do you remember anything at all?"

Josiah stared at her, then looked past her as Old Wiley approached. He shook his head. "Not really." He stopped speaking, distress on his face. "I can't remember."

"Do you know your name?"

"It's…" He stopped, a puzzled look on his face. "It's….." He stopped again, his gaze going to his hands. "I'm married?"

Old Wiley stood behind his daughter as she sat assessing Josiah. "We found the band in your pocket.   We're assuming it's yours."

Josiah stared at it, a picture of a woman's hand placing it on his finger coming to mind. "I can remember it being put there, but I can't remember her." He looked up, distress once more on his face. "Why not?"

Suzie and her father shared a glance, and Old Wiley finally nodded.

"We need to tell him, Suzie. Tad won't be back for a day or so and we need to get this young fellow up and on his feet as soon as we can."

Josiah stared at the two of them. "What's going on? What do you have to tell me?" He coughed and swallowed against the dryness in his throat, accepting the mug of water handed him once again.

"We know who you are, but we weren't sure if you would remember. Dad's asked you over the past week or so you've been here who you are and you haven't been able to tell him. When Dad found you, you had no identification on you, other than that ring tucked down in your pocket. This is what we know."

Suzie spoke rapidly, giving concise details, then turned to her father, who stared at Josiah for a moment.

Josiah spoke. "So what you're telling me is that I can't remember who I am, that I was kidnapped and was then involved in a car accident, and from that accident, got lost in the woods? That sounds like something from a book or a movie."

"It's what happened, Josiah. Suzie's husband is a member of our local police force and was searching for you. Suzie's a search and rescue coordinator as well and searched for you. It was Roadie and I who found you, got you back here, and nursed you."

Josiah held up his hand. "Roadie?"

Suzie laughed. "His horse. Mom named him that."

Josiah laid his head back, exhausted. "I need to think this through." He raised his head again. "My wife? Who is she? And where is she?"

Again the two exchanged a glance. "Suzie's husband's working on that. He'll be back up in a day or so. We'll know more when he comes back. Our main concern is to get you up on your feet and strong enough to leave." Old Wiley looked at him, compassion filling his face. "We'd get you to her but the only way in or out is by foot or horse, and you're just not up to that right now."

Josiah sighed, knowing the old man was right. "I know. But I feel like there's a lot of danger somewhere, and it's directed at my wife." He stumbled over the words, not quite sure if they were true. His eyes closed before he could say anything more and he slept.

Suzie watched for a few minutes, then stood, speaking with her father. "We need to get him out of here, Dad, and soon."

"I know, Suzie, I know." He walked over to the wood stove, stirring up the coals and adding more wood, drawing the coffee pot forward. "It worries me, you being here."

"So far, we're fine, Dad. Yours is a hard place to find unless you know the exact location. I find it interesting that he didn't remember being married."

"That makes me think it's recent." Old Wiley stood, staring at the rough log walls of his home. "Did Tad say when he would be back up?"

She shook her head. "In the next day or so. But Josiah's not going to be ready to move by then."

Old Wiley turned to his daughter. "What aren't you saying, Suzie?"

She shook her head. "It's just he's very weak and I'm not how he would do on the trek out. It can be rough." She laid her hand on her father's arm. "What are you thinking, Dad?"

"I'm thinking that there's likely a young woman out there grieving for her man, and he'll start grieving soon too. We need to get them back together." He turned, pacing the cabin, then walked out, leaving Suzie staring after him, then turning back to stand and watch Josiah.

Two days later, Tad walked into the cabin and looked around. Josiah was not in the bunk. So, where was he?

He turned as he felt an arm come around him. Suzie stood there, a pleased smile on her face.

"Tad. You're here!"

"I am, sweetheart. Now, where are Wiley and his guest?"

"Out back. They've been having a pretty heated discussion, those two."

Tad grinned. "He's ready to go, is he?"

She nodded. "His mind says he is, his body says otherwise. By tomorrow, I don't think we're going to be able to hold him here. He'll head out walking and end up getting lost again."

"What does Wiley say?"

"He's not happy that Josiah is pushing to leave. He knows how rough the trip would be on him."

Tad sighed. "Then, I guess I need to go talk to those two. Andrew called me two days ago. Things have escalated with Faith."

"How?"

Tad pointed to the outdoors. "Let's go find the two and bring Josiah up to date." He paused, looking down at his wife. "Has he remembered anything at all?"

She shook her head. "Not much, but it's starting to clear. I think maybe if we get him back to his normal habitat, it might trigger something."

He nodded, then pointed once more to the door, stopping to grab a mug of coffee on the way by. He stood outside the cabin, watching as Old Wiley and Josiah faced off against each other. He could tell that Josiah was not real steady on his feet yet, but the determination to leave was there. He looked at his father-in-law and saw the compassion and caring in his face.

"Wiley. Josiah. How be you both come back here and sit? I've some news but I also need to make some plans with you." Tad watched as they both glanced at him, then back at each other. His head dropped as he shook it, hiding the grin that quickly went across his face.

Suzie stood, hands on hips. "Do what you're told, both of you. I swear, you both are acting like two Banty roosters, both determined to rule the roost."

"And just what would you know about Banty roosters, my dear?" Old Wiley's hand was out to steady Josiah as they made their way back to the cabin. "Sit, Josiah. Here's some water. You need to drink more than you are."

"Stop telling me what I do or don't need, Wiley." Josiah took the water, a disgruntled look on his face.

"Sniping at each other won't help, Josiah." Tad waited until the younger man faced him. "I need to talk with you. Tell me what you remember."

Josiah's eyes took on a faraway look and he stilled. "Not a lot, I'm sorry to say." He twisted the ring on his finger, staring at it. "I don't do manual labour, my hands don't show that." He looked up at Tad, fear and discomfort in his eyes. "I get bits and pieces and flashes. Like this." He held up his hand. "I can see the ring being placed, but I don't know the woman."

Tad nodded. "It's understandable, Josiah. From what I have determined, you were knocked unconscious, stuffed into a car and driven from your home.   That car was then in an accident, leaving the road and ramming into a tree. It is a wonder that you all survived." He got the look on Josiah's face. "There were three men with you, your kidnappers. We have them in custody, but they're not talking."

He pulled out some photos from his pocket, studied them, then handed the top one to Josiah. "This first one is your family. Your Dad, your mom, and your brother and sister.   Twins, I understand, who are two years younger than you." Josiah studied it, vague memories trying to surface.

"This one is a group of your friends, taken last summer, your friend Zeke said. Their names are on the back."   Josiah flipped it over, his lips moving as he silently read the names.

"I can sort of remember these guys." He looked up and at the other photos in Tad's hands. "What else do you have?"

"This is the uncle of the woman you married. You have been living in their work shop for the last couple of months."

"In their work shop? Why?"

"We'll come to that in a moment." Tad stared down at the last photo, not sure how to approach it. "This is Faith Lockwood, your wife." He handed over the photo.

Josiah took it, apprehension on his face, his hand shaking. His eyes stared into the forest, not seeing the sunlight flickering down through the thick canopy, the leaves and branches moving slightly with the breeze. He didn't hear the call of the birds, the sounds of the stream or the frogs or the insects. This was a moment he wanted to move through so badly, he thought, but it would change everything he knew at that moment. Lord, do I believe in You? Are You walking through this with me? I can't do it alone. These are just new friends who don't know what happened in the past. Only You do at this moment.

He gripped the photo, then turned his eyes to it, the fingers of his other hand reaching to trace the young woman's face.

"Faith!" The three with him barely caught his words. "Oh, Faith! What have they done?" He looked up briefly before his eyes slid closed and his body slipped from his chair.

Tad was there to catch him before he hit the ground, turning to walk back into the cabin to place him on the bunk. Suzie reached for Josiah's wrist.

"His pulse is okay. I think it's just shock, Tad."

Old Wiley spoke from where he stood, watching. "He's remembered what's been going on, I would suspect."

Tad nodded. "He has. Now, I didn't get to finish what I need to say and I have to be out of here before nightfall."

"Do you have plans in place, you and Andrew?" Suzie stood, her hand on her husband's arm.

"We do. It's just a matter of getting Josiah to where we need him."

Chapter 18

$\mathscr{B}$ill looked up at the knock on the front door of the shop and walked through. Andrew stood there, eyes scanning the area. He unlocked it and Andrew slipped in, quiet words spoken between the two. Bill nodded, then headed out the door to find Tom. April was catching some rest to be ready for duty that night.

Andrew paused in the doorway, watching the activity going on. He knew Faith's business had markedly increased but he hadn't realized how much. He sighed to himself. Now, how was he ever going to be able to take her away from this?

He waited until Faith stepped back from the pattern she was laying out and spoke. She spun, startled, eyes questioning why he was there again so soon.

"Andrew?" Her question was soft but it caught everyone's attention.

"Faith, we need to move you now."

"Move me? Where to? I can't leave. I have too many orders to work on." She stared behind her at the work table and the pile of orders waiting.

"Faith, Child, if Andrew says you have to go, you'll have to." Seth moved to stand beside her. "The threat has escalated, I take it, Andrew?"

"It has. We need to get Faith out of here now. They've gone to the streets looking for someone to nab her for them." Andrew watched the faces turned to him. "Faith, you won't have time to pack anything. We need to leave now. April and Tom will stay here with your uncle and Silas. Beth, it's your decision whether you keep coming out or not."

Beth nodded. "I have no fear, Andrew. If Faith's not here, someone has to work on the orders for her. Faith, leave your patterns up on the computer. Seth can pull them for me as we need them. Will's heading this way as well and he can help." She turned to Seth. "Given what's happening, I would say we need to stay here with you."

Seth nodded. "I think so. Silas?"

Silas shook his head. "I'm not leaving until I see Josiah. I may not be able to do the soldering, but I can certainly cut glass and cut the lead came for you."

"All right, then. Let's move out then, Faith. Wait." He turned as he heard the door and Bill and Tom appeared behind him. He moved away to confer with them, his eyes watching the four in the work room. He shook his head at something Tom said, then paced through to the front door of the store.

Seth moved to stand beside the two officers. "Bill, what's happening?"

"We didn't get Faith out of here in time, Seth. Whoever it is has men all around us."

"So now what?" Seth turned to watch his niece, who stood, arms wrapped around herself, fear evident on her face.

"Andrew is trying to come up with a way to get Faith out of here, but it's going to be tricky. I'm not even sure we can."

"We have to, Bill. There is no way I want her in the hands of those men. I can tell you right now, we would never see her alive again." He stepped forward so he could watch Andrew. "Whatever happened with Brownlee?"

"That's what triggered this, we think. He and his three cohorts were arrested this morning. Young Brownlee was arrested to for tampering with evidence. Yours is not the first case this has happened with. Andrew's been asked to take over the force here for now until we can get everything sorted out."

Seth nodded. "So they've lost their protection from the force as well, have that? That changes everything now, doesn't it?"

"Have you come up with a plan, Bill?" Andrew had walked back to join them.

Bill shook his head. "Not yet, Andrew. I really don't know how we'll do it."

A voice spoke from behind them, causing them to turn. Silas had moved up without them hearing him.

"So what I understand you to say is that Faith is at greater risk now than she was and you need to find a way to get her out of here without them seeing her leave?" He turned to pace. "April and Faith are about the same size and colouring right?"

The men nodded, Bill and Andrew's eyes lighting up at Silas' words. "If we get Faith back to the house, then we can send April out, dressed as Faith, with Tom and maybe they'll follow them."

Andrew paced. "I'm not sure that would work, Silas. I doubt they would all follow the one car."

Silas nodded. "I know they won't. How many are there out there, do you think?"

"At least four that we can determine. I have officers moving in behind them, but I can't guarantee we'll have them all."

Sudden shouts and the sound of gunfire caused Andrew, Bill, and Tom to spin and head for the door. Bill and Tom left, weapons in hand, April running towards them from the house. Andrew locked the door and stood, eyes watchful. He knew it could well be a trap to get to Faith.

Seth moved up behind him. "Is that them, Andrew?"

Andrew nodded. "I suspect so, Seth. Is the back door locked?"

"It is and Silas installed a metal grate to pull across once we locked the door. They can't get in through the door. The windows, now that's a difference matter, but I don't think they'd risk that in the daylight. He's working on doing the same grates for the windows."

"Depends on how desperate they are." Andrew squinted, watching as his officers moved forward, shoving men in front of them., Bill heading back his way. Andrew unlocked the door, and Bill slipped inside.

"Talk to me, Bill."

"You were right. They were waiting for night to move in. They had their plans all laid out, nice and neat on a paper. Someone really didn't plan this well." He paused, staring back out the door. "I think this was a diversion, though, Andrew. It just doesn't feel right."

"I know. Tell you what. We'll send Faith out in your car among these cruisers. Once we get her to our station, we can go from there." He walked back quickly to

Faith. "Faith, grab what you need from here. We're moving you out now."

Faith shot him a quick glance, then reached for her jacket, purse and the knapsack Bill had ordered her to pack with essentials and keep with her at all times. Quick hugs to the ones staying behind and Bill had her across the parking lot and stuffed into the front seat of his car, pulling out with the rest of the cruisers.

Seth watched, despair filling him, his heart lifting in prayer for safety for Faith and Josiah and a swift resolution to the fight.

Faith stared in front of her and then behind her. "Bill, what's going on?"

"We've tucked you into the line of cruisers. These are taking the men we arrested back to our station. Once we're there, we'll tuck you into Andrew's office for now. He and Tad are coming up with plans for you and Josiah."

"Have you heard how Josiah is?"

Bill shook his head. "Not in the last few days. Tad's not saying much, trying to keep it as quiet as he can that Josiah is still alive."

Faith sat back. "That's good, I guess. Will Uncle Seth be okay?"

"More than likely. They won't use him to get to you; they know they can't."

"How do they know that?"

Bill sent her a quick look. "Because he fought this out years ago, when you were small. And whoever it is has been around for at least that long."

"That long? How?"

Bill shrugged as he checked his mirrors. "We have information that we're not sharing right now as we work through what's happened in your town. We've arrested the chief and some of his officers as well as some town people in the last twenty-four hours. What you are involved in goes really deep, Faith. It's not just about money any more, as I think you understand."

She nodded. "I kind of got that when that last letter was delivered. It's about revenge against my family, and others have gotten pulled in." She shivered, fear coursing through her. "Can I stay safe, though, Bill?"

"We're going to do our best to make sure that happens. We're also working on getting you and Josiah back together again. So, tell me, what made you two decide to elope?"

She stared at him, mouth open, then caught the teasing glint in his eye. She shrugged, a smile on her face. "We were going to wait but decided life's too short and uncertain. We had peace about our decision. And in case you're wondering who, we talked to Zeke's minister and he was glad to perform the ceremony. Josiah's made his peace again with the Lord." She stopped speaking, face turning to the window. Bill caught the tears on her cheek she couldn't control.

"We'll do our best, Faith, to both keep you safe and get you and Josiah back together."

She nodded, unable to speak, watching as Bill entered the secured area behind the police building. He slid from behind the wheel, searching the area, then coming around to open her door, catching her knapsack for her. Hand to her back, he rushed her into the building and to Andrew's office.

"You're safe here for now, Faith. Lock the door behind me. I have a key to the door and so does Andrew. No one else can get in."

She nodded, fear once more coursing through her. She paced, her thoughts drifting to Josiah. Where is he, Lord? Is he safe? Has he healed? I know You're the strong tower we run to when we're afraid, that You gather us up under Your wings. That's what we need right now.

She finally sat on the leather couch, laying her head back. Fatigue was catching up with her. She raised her head, searching the room, finally spotting the little fridge Andrew had tucked in a corner. She opened, finding bottles of water and juice. She knew he wouldn't mind if she had one.

She returned to the couch, this time laying down. Her sleep had been spotty for so long now, the fatigue felt like it was part of her bones. Her eyes drifted closed and she slept, not hearing Bill as he entered to ask her something. He stood for a moment, then reached for the blanket folded up on the lower shelf of the bookcase and spread it over her.

Andrew paused in the doorway, his eyes on Faith, then raised to Bill. "Has she been sleeping long?"

Bill turned, shrugging. "I don't think so, but I don't want to wake her if I can help it."

"We'll need to Bill. I've talked to Tad. They have Josiah back down the mountain. We're working on getting the two back together again." He ran his hand down his face, tiredness evident on it, then sank into his chair, his eyes once more going to Faith. "We'll let her sleep for now. What have you got?"

"Not a lot. The five men we arrested aren't talking, but they're all from her town. Two are business owners, three are from the streets and have records."

"Business owners? Now, isn't that interesting."

"I would suspect somehow they've been blackmailed or coerced into today. They were really quick to give up. In fact, I don't think they would have taken part in anything today. The officers who arrested them said they were turning away from the area and heading for a vehicle."

"Cracks in the group, is there? That's encouraging. Any word on who the leader is?"

Bill shook his head. "Nothing concrete. The chief and the ones we arrested earlier aren't talking."

"Somehow, I didn't think they would." Andrew rose and went to the door as a knock came. A quick word of conference, and he peeked back around the door at Faith, sighing as he did so.

"What's happened, Andrew?" Bill spoke as Andrew shut the door, then stood his hand resting on it.

"The chief has been killed in the jail yard in Oak City. We're trying to figure out who and how, but someone got to him."

Bill watched as Andrew walked back to his desk and stood, fingers tapping on the desktop. "This changes everything, Bill. Do we have a dirty cop here or there?"

Bill drew a deep breath. "It's highly possible and more than likely. Which means, they know Faith is here."

Andrew nodded as he raised his head, his eyes meeting Bill. "We thought we had her safe. Now, I'm not so sure."

Bill stood and paced. "Where do we go then, Andrew?"

Andrew sat, elbows on his desk, and rested his chin on his linked hands. "We'll have to come up with a new plan and quickly.

Chapter 19

$\mathcal{J}$osiah stood at the kitchen counter in the house he had been taken to, staring at the water as it dripped down into the coffee pot. Is this what I've come to, Lord, just standing watching water drip, waiting for a cup of coffee? There has to be more I can do, more to help Faith, to find the men responsible. He turned as he heard footsteps behind him.

Tad stood in the kitchen doorway, hands jammed into his jeans' pockets, a thoughtful look on his face. He was hesitant to say anything to Josiah, but he knew he had to. Andrew had called with word about Brownlee. Things were escalating. Lord, where do we go from here? I know You have a plan and a purpose. I just don't see it.

"Tad. What word do you have on Faith?" Josiah turned to study the man standing in the doorway.

Tad walked over and poured a cup of the freshly-brewed coffee, then pointed at the table. "Sit, Josiah. We need to talk."

"About what?" Josiah's hands cupped his mug as his eyes watched Tad.

"First, Chief Brownlee was arrested for the murders of Faith's parents and Noah's mother. As well, some other officers and some businessmen were arrested. However, someone got to him in the jail yard. He's dead." Tad looked up to find Josiah's eyes steady on him. "Now about your wife. Faith is safe so far. Andrew and Bill have her tucked away in what they are hoping is a safe spot. Someone made a move today to get her."

Josiah nodded, rubbing the back of his neck. "But that's not all, is it, Tad?"

"No, it's not." Tad stared past Josiah, his eyes on the window behind him. "She received another letter two days ago. The game has changed. Whoever it is wants Faith now, not money."

"What!" Josiah's explosive comment ripped through the kitchen as he shoved his chair back and stood, pacing in an agitated manner. "Who is this guy?"

"Andrew believes it's related to her parents' death. Whoever it is now wants revenge for what she has refused to pay."

Josiah turned agonized eyes to Tad. "Please keep her safe."

Tad nodded. "That's what we're planning on doing. We're trying to work it out to get the two of you back together, but our plans are still fluctuating, given what's been happening. Her uncle stayed at the shop along with Bill, is it? His parents stayed. Your father's there as well. They're working on keeping the orders fulfilled." Tad paused, then spoke slowly. "I heard you set up a website for a group." He held up his hand as Josiah turned, ready to deny it. "It's okay. Faith told Bill to tell me. Talk to me about it."

Josiah stared at him, not quite sure now if he could trust Tad. "No. It's not mine to tell."

Frustrated, Tad stood, walked to the front of the house and then back. "It could mean your lives, Josiah."

Josiah shook his head. "No. I want to talk to Faith and Bill." He knew Tad was frustrated, but there was no way he would speak of something like these, something he had done in confidence. He knew word was getting out, but he still didn't feel that he could open up about it.

Tad finally nodded and pulled out his phone as it chimed.

"Andrew. We were just talking about you, Josiah and me. What's happening on your end? I see. That would make a difference, wouldn't it? All right, then. I'll see what I can do about getting him there. It will take some arranging. Josiah will want to know how Faith is? Good. No, he's fine, just not cooperating the way I would like him to. No, he hasn't said a word about that, just asked for Faith. Okay. Give me an hour, then call back." He thoughtfully pocketed his phone and looked up at Josiah. "Faith is fine, so far. Andrew and Bill will need to move her and I think I'll need to move you too. There have been some leaks somewhere in one of our departments, even though very few people have known what's been going on."

Josiah nodded. "That's about what I figured. You can't hide people and not have them missed." He stopped. "Hiding people.

You always stick them away somewhere, don't you, and put a guard on them?"

Tad nodded, wondering where Josiah was going with this.

"Then, hide us in plain sight."

"In plain sight?" Tad choked on his mouthful of coffee. "In plain sight? And how do we do that? With your height, you're not exactly easy to miss."

Josiah laughed, an idea gathering steam. He spoke quickly, Tad staring at him in dismay at first and then in a more thoughtful manner.

"It might work, you know. It just might work. But how do we get what we need?"

"Talk to Zeke's minister. They have a lot of equipment that they gather for missions. Surely he would have something there we could use."

Tad shook his finger at Josiah. "I like how you think, Josiah. It just might be what we need to do. It's risky though."

Josiah nodded. "I know it is. We would need to figure out what town to put us in, and then bring in trusted officers from another force. Unless you know of a private security firm that could provide us protection."

Tad shook his head. "Too risky. The private security teams in our area are too well known. It would be a giveaway if one of them suddenly showed up."

Tad pulled out his phone, frowning as he did so. "Will Faith go along with this?" When Josiah didn't answer, he looked up at him. "Josiah, will she? I need to know what you think before I call Andrew back."

Josiah sighed, then pushed back from the table, going to stand in front of the patio doors, staring out into the gathering gloom.

"Come away from there, Josiah. You're a target standing in front of the doors."

Josiah spun and walked back to the table. "I thought you said we were safe here."

"We are, but given what's happening, I can't guarantee that someone hasn't found us." Tad stared at Josiah. "Again, will Faith go along with this?"

Josiah shrugged. "I'm sure she will. She wants this over as much or more than I do. She needs it over to come to terms with the fact that her parents and aunt were murdered, that she and her uncle have been threatened and that we want to move on with our lives and can't with this hanging over us, not really, I guess."

Tad nodded, knowing how he would have felt had it been Suzie and himself. "All right. Let me call Andrew and put the plan to him. I can't guarantee he'll go for it though. Andrew. I've talked to Josiah. He's come up with a wild plan." Tad spoke quickly and succinctly, letting Andrew know what Josiah wanted to do.

Andrew sighed, looking over at Faith, who was still sleeping, then at Bill. "Let me wake up Faith and talk to her. I'll call you back."

Andrew thoughtfully studied the young woman sleeping on his couch, then raised his eyes to Bill. "Josiah's come up with a wild plan. I need to wake Faith up to talk to her about it and I hate to do that. She needs her sleep."

Bill nodded, then turned at movement from the couch as Faith roused, then sat up, pushing her hair back from her face.

"Faith?" Andrew's voice was quiet as he spoke her name, his eyes watchful. "Are you awake enough to talk with us?"

She nodded, then reached for the bottle of water she had taken from the fridge earlier. "I am. Now what?" She had a disgruntled tone in her voice, causing Bill to quickly hide the grin that came to his face.

"I just spoke with Tad." He held up a hand as she went to speak. "Josiah is fine, anxious to be with you. We're trying to work that out." He stopped speaking, his eyes locking with Bill's before he sighed and looked back at her.

Faith watched the silent communication between the two men, then spoke. "What plan have you come up with that I know I won't like?"

Andrew shook his finger at her. "Hear us out first, okay? And it's not our plan. It comes from Josiah. Tad and I are willing to consider it, if we can't come up with anything different." He quickly explained what Josiah had come up with, watching for a reaction from Faith.

She nodded slowly as she raised the water bottle to take another drink, her eyes thoughtful but not focused on the men in the room with her. "It will work. Put us into another town, a larger one where we can get lost." Her eyes turned to watch Andrew. "You haven't come up with anything yet, I can tell."

"No, we haven't yet, Faith. There's also something else. The chief has been murdered."

She shrugged. "I feel sorry for his wife, but he would have faced judgement and a protracted trial with his lawyer trying to get him off."

Bill and Andrew shared a look. This was not the response they expected from Faith.

"Faith?" Bill spoke.

She looked up at him. "What? I'm sorry. He's an evil man and caused the death of my parents. What do you expect me to say?"

Bill shrugged. "Just don't let your trust in God slip, okay?"

She nodded. "It hasn't, Bill. We're told not to avenge, that God avenges for us. Maybe this is what happened. God allowed this, Bill and Andrew. He could have prevented it, you know."

The men nodded. Then Andrew rose and walked out of the room, a thought coming to him. Bill watched him walk away, then turned to Faith.

"Where do we go then, Faith? You're willing to put your life into the plan Josiah dreamed up?"

"I am, and for the record, he didn't "dream it up", to quote you. God gave it to him." She looked around. "Do you have paper and a pen? I need to give you a list and you'll need to find what we need, unless you'll let me go shopping."

"That's not happening, Faith. I'll get Joanna to help. She's been itching to get involved."

Chapter 20

*J*osiah had been moved again to another house in another town. He was tired, not quite over his injuries from the accident and his kidnapping. He paced the living room of the house he had been tucked into, Tad watching from the living room doorway.

Hearing a vehicle and then car doors, Tad moved to the front door, watching through the side window. He opened the door with a quiet voice, then pointed to the living room.

Faith stopped in the doorway, her eyes on her husband, hands to her mouth. He was alive, a little battered looking, but he was here. She didn't say anything, just stood and watched.

Josiah stopped his pacing, a sense of being watched by someone new coming over him. Friend or foe, he wondered?

Turning, he stopped and his eyes slid shut. Faith was across the room and into his arms before he could open his eyes again.

Tad and Andrew watched, then headed for the kitchen, their voices quiet as they talked over their plans. Bill had tucked what they had needed into Andrew's trunk. They both knew it would mean moving the two again, but that was a chance they would have to take.

"Are we good here for the night, Tad?"

Tad shook his head. "No, we need to move them again. This was just a temporary stop. I still think we should just put them somewhere they can't be found."

"And where would that be? Bill has had word that every safe house we have has been searched by someone. And he's getting word that the same is true for your safe houses."

"What?" Tad was shocked. "We have leaks all over the place, don't we?"

Andrew nodded. "It would appear that way. Or at least one leak that knows where all the safe houses are. It looks as if we'll have to move them somewhere else."

Tad nodded as his eyes roamed the kitchen. "We need to be cautious how we talk about anything, I'm thinking, Andrew. I searched the house when we came in, but I'm not confident there isn't a listening device hidden somewhere I didn't find."

Andrew nodded. "That's what I'm thinking too, Tad." He rose from his seat at the table and walked towards the living room. "Let's get those two out of here."

Faith turned in Josiah's arms as the two officers returned to the living room, her eyes searching their faces, then her heart dropping as she read them. Stern lines had deepened on their faces.

"No, I'm not leaving Josiah. Not again." Tears were close to the surface and evident in her voice, as Josiah's arms tightened around her.

"We're not separating you two. We're moving you. We've had word that all our safe houses are compromised."

"All of them?" Josiah's eyes narrowed and a grim look came over his face. "Where now? I still think we'd be safer on the street."

Tad nodded as Andrew spoke. "You may well be safer there. Bill's gotten what we need for you in my car trunk. We just need to get you to some place where you can change."

"Try Zeke's church, Andrew. The pastor there will let us. He's worked in some pretty tough areas of towns, as a street pastor." Josiah tilted his head to look at Faith. "I hate to take Faith to the streets though."

Faith shook her head. "If it works, Josiah, it's what will do."

"Well, then, if that's what you want to do, then let's go. Here. These are some pay-as-you go phones that don't track back to anyone of us. Keep them and only use them as you need to. We would ask that you keep in touch with one of us once a day. Alternate who you call."

Hours later, Josiah watched as Faith finished tucking her auburn hair up into a bun and pulling on a wig of short spiked blond hair. He knew she had already inserted the brown contacts, changing her eye colour. He had done the same, changing his eye colour to gray. He had shaved his beard, something Faith hadn't wanted him to do, but one thing they felt had been necessary. She had helped to dye his hair red.

"Now then, you two, are you set?" Andrew watched from the doorway of the room they had changed in. "I still don't like this."

"Andrew, who would look for us in a homeless shelter or living on the streets? They certainly aren't going to be looking for Josiah in that." Faith pointed at the worn wheelchair Zeke's pastor, Aaron, had unearthed for them.

Tad shook his head as he entered the room. "It's risky, Faith. I wish you would have not agreed to this."

Faith spun on him. "It's our lives, Tad. God is in control. No matter where we are or who we're with, He will be there with us."

Tad took a step back, then nodded. "All right. Then we're out of here. Aaron, thank you for stepping up to help."

"Not a problem, Tad. If you need to contact them, contact me. I work in the downtown area and the homeless shelters as well. I can find them."

Andrew also nodded. "Thank you. You two, stay safe. It's not over, not by a long shot. I don't want to be the one to inform your people that something happened to you. As it is, I'm going to have to tell them you're not in protective custody but out on your own."

Faith and Josiah exchanged a look, then watched as the two men walked away. Aaron studied the two remaining in the room and offered up a prayer for safety and swift resolution of the problem they faced. Problem, he snorted to himself. More like a life and death battle.

Hours later, Josiah paused, his hands cramping from pushing the wheelchair tires. He looked around, tired and frustrated.

"Josiah?" Faith spoke from his side. "We need to come up with new names. That's the one thing we didn't do, did we?"

Josiah leaned his head back and watched the face of the lady he loved. "No, we didn't, sweetheart. That's the one part of the plan we didn't work out, isn't it?"

"It is." She turned, then pushed his chair towards a park bench. "Let's sit here for a moment. I need to get off my feet."

They sat in silence, the peace of the park calming them.

"So what do we call one another?" Josiah spoke, his eyes roaming the park.

"We could always just say sweetheart or honey, but we need names to give the shelter, I think." She sat back, dismay in her demeanour. "What names do we use that we'll remember?"

"How about Peter and Annie?"

She nodded. "That's good. But will we remember?"

"We have to. Our lives depend on it." He sighed. "I don't like this, you know. But with the safe houses compromised, we don't have much choice."

"No. I'm not sure though that we'll be much safer here on the streets." She turned as a woman approached, her clothes dirty and worn.

"You're new to town?" Her teeth, what remained of them, were stained and broken. "I know of a good shelter you can go to. Follow me."

Faith and Josiah exchanged glances. Then Faith spoke. "We're going to stay here for a while. Just tell us where it is."

The woman stared at them, then shook her head and moved away, mumbling to herself.

"That was strange. It's like it was a set up, Josiah."

He nodded. "I know. Let's get moving. I suddenly don't feel so safe any more."

"Wait. We need to come up with a plan of where we can go to, a hiding place if you will, where we can wait for help to reach us."

"Aaron's church. He'll give us sanctuary until Tad and Andrew can get to us."

Faith turned and looked around her. "I can feel someone out there, Josiah. Somehow, I don't think this was such a good plan, after all."

"Let's find somewhere we can get something to eat and then somewhere to shelter for the night. I'd rather not head for the shelter today if I can help it. If anyone suspects that's what we're doing, they'll start searching them tonight. Even with our disguises, I don't think we'll avoid them forever."

"I know. I just hope Andrew finds them before they find us."

The woman straightened and watched as the two moved away, her eyes thoughtful. Now, who were those two? They certainly didn't want her help. She shrugged. It was none of her business, now was it? She looked down at the hand she had pulled from the torn pocket and the money she had gripped in it. It was enough she could move to another town. That's what she would do.

The man waited at the shelter, watching for the woman he had contacted to come back. She had disappeared. He cursed, knowing that he would never see her again. He searched the men and women lining up for their meal and then walked away. He knew those two were in this town, he had followed their vehicle. But where were they? He had managed to get into the church and searched it. They weren't there and hadn't left with the officers. He had talked to the minister but hadn't gotten any information from him.

Chapter 21

$\mathcal{A}$ week later, Josiah paused outside a restaurant. He had quickly found out which ones were wheelchair friendly and which ones wouldn't let in homeless people. He sighed. How did a person change the mentality out there? God, only you can. Please let us go home soon. I'm tired of this.

Faith studied the restaurant. "We won't be able to go in there, you know."

Josiah nodded, then spoke, frustration evident. "I never knew how hard it was to be handicapped. Let's move on and find somewhere we can get something to eat." He turned his chair, stopping to watch her face. "How is our money hanging out?"

She sighed. "We'll need to get some more somehow in the next few days." She bit her lower lip. "I wish this was over, sweetheart. I want to go home."

He nodded, his eyes watchful as he looked around. "Didn't Aaron say they were having a lunch today at the church? Maybe we can sneak in there."

She smiled slightly. "I'm sure we can, but do we want to? Too many people would remember seeing us."

"Let's head that way, and then you can go find him."

The man walking by them, stopped and turned, a frown on his face. He then turned and followed them, studying them, finally nodding. His phone out and a call made, he continued on the same path they had taken.

Faith felt the eyes on her back and hesitated, finally pushing Josiah into a store.

"Faith?" Josiah's voice was low but held a question.

"We've picked up a shadow, Josiah. I think our cover's been blown." Faith watched over the racks of clothing as the man entered, his eyes searching for them. She ducked back down. "We need to get out of here by the back door and now. You'll have to leave the wheelchair at the door, sweetheart." She pushed him through the employees only door and to the back door, cracking it open to peek out. "Come on. I think we'll be okay."

Josiah grabbed her hand and pulled her with him, the wheelchair abandoned. He searched the area, but couldn't see anyone. He shoved her into a darkened deep doorway and waited. He could hear the running footsteps coming their way.

"Where'd they go? I know it was them."

They could hear the men searching. Josiah looked frantically around, then tried the door behind Faith. It cracked open, and he shoved her through, then grabbing her hand, pulled her towards the front of the building, bursting out into the busy street. They mingled with the crowd, but knew that they were likely to be spotted. Josiah's height made that a given. For once, he wished he was under six foot, instead of standing at six foot three. He hadn't seen a lot of men his height in his time down there.

"We need to get in touch with Andrew or Tad, Josiah." Faith was having trouble getting her words out, she was out of breath.

He nodded. "I know. We need to find somewhere safe to do that though." He turned to look behind him and groaned. "We haven't lost them yet. Where can we go?"

Faith searched the area, then pointed. "There, down that alley. It leads, I think, to a park where we can lose them, I hope, and head for the church. Surely Aaron can help us."

"Do we want to involve him?"

"We already have." She turned as they ran, her hand in Josiah's strong grip. "I don't see them, yet."

Josiah slid to a stop at the end of the alley and peeked out. "Looks clear so far. Let's go. Can you run a bit more?"

"I don't have a choice, do I?"

They ran for the trees, losing themselves there and then, getting their bearings, heading for Aaron's church at a fast walk.

"They're not the men who were after us before, are they?"

Josiah shook his head at Faith's question. "No, they're not." He stopped and groaned again, pointing at the church parking lot. "Look, they must have known we'd head this way." He pulled Faith back into the trees and reached for his phone.

"Wait, don't call Andrew or Tad. I have a feeling someone's been watching or listening to them." She paced and then spun. "I know who we can call." She pulled out her phone and dialed from memory. "Hi. It's Faith. We really need your help. We're in Logan City, near the community church. Yes, the one that Aaron pastors. We have men after us, and you're our only hope."

Josiah threw a questioning look at Faith. "Who did you call?"

"A friend. You'll recognize him, I think. Do you remember the two men who were silent when the group talked to us?"

Josiah nodded, wondering where she was heading with that.

"One of them came to see me when you were gone. I recognized him, but he wouldn't confirm or deny it. I trust him, Josiah. At least I hope we can."

She turned to watch the church and the three men pacing outside it. "We can't get to Aaron. Do you have his number?"

"No, but it's on the sign if I can get a picture of it with this phone. There. Now to enlarge it." He squinted as he read off the numbers to her.

"Aaron? It's Faith. We were coming to you for help, but the men after us are outside the church. Yes, I know. Someone found us somehow. No, don't do that. I don't want you to put yourself at risk." Faith listened as Aaron tried to come up with a plan. "Please, call Andrew or Tad. Let them know what happened. I don't dare do that. I have a friend coming for us. At least, I hope it's a friend." She abruptly cut the call and dropped the phone into her pocket after turning it off. "Turn off your phone for now, Josiah. Aaron will likely try to call you and we don't want that."

Andrew turned at both Bill and Tad approached him as he waited in line at the local coffee shop. He didn't like the looks on their faces. He stepped from the line, deciding that his coffee would just have to wait.

"What's up, Bill?   I don't like those looks."

"Someone spotted Josiah and Faith. They've had to ditch their disguises. Aaron called.   Faith called him but they couldn't get into the church.   Somehow, the men found out about Aaron and were watching the church. Aaron said Faith had called in a friend."

"A friend? Now who would that be?" Andrew was getting angry and needed to tamp that down, he knew.   "So where are they now?"

Tad shrugged.   "We have no idea. They've turned their phones off.   When I call it goes straight to voice mail."

"Bill, you're on your way.   Civilian clothes and your own vehicle, please.   Tad, come.   Let's go call Aaron and see if he's heard anything else."

Bill turned for the door, then stopped. "Where do I find them, Andrew?   Do we know?"

Tad shook his head. "I heard they were at Zeke's church, but that they may not be there now. I have no idea who the friend is they went to. I wish they hadn't done that."

"They're not sure who they can trust at this point, Tad. I can't say as I blame them." Andrew watched as Tad paced, deep in thought. "What are you thinking, Tad?"

"How many of us knew where they'd be?"

"If you're suspecting Bill, don't. He's too good a cop and too good a friend to Josiah to have done anything to jeopardize his safety. And I know he wouldn't have talked to anyone. Their people had no idea where they were."

Tad slumped down into a chair. "I know, Andrew. I'm just thinking it through." He ran his hands through his short black hair. "Someone had to think it through like we did and put out word that they were wanted. Did we give it away by not putting them in a safe house?"

"I doubt it. More than likely someone followed us somehow and saw us leave the church without them."

Tad nodded. "That's likely how it went." The chiming of his phone caught his attention. "It's Josiah. Josiah? Are you safe? You are. Good. Now where are you? Still at the church? Who's coming? Now, wait a minute. Angus? From Faith's town?" He turned to look at Andrew, who nodded. "Andrew knows him. Why him? I see. Wait, Josiah. How does she know she can trust him? You can't or won't say. Listen, we need to get you two to somewhere safe. Josiah? Josiah?" Tad could hear scuffling from over the phone, then the sound of the phone falling. The connection was lost.

"Something just happen, Tad?" Andrew was on his feet.

"It did, and it doesn't sound good. I don't think this Andrew made it to them in time. We've lost them." Tad spun and headed for the door. "We need to get in touch with the chief in Logan City. I'm heading that way. You with me?"

"Absolutely." He was out the door after Tad, looking for Bill. "Bill, you're with us. Now!"

Bill had changed to civilian clothes and was headed for his car. Turning, he ran after Tad and Andrew. "What's up?"

Tad spoke. "I got a call from Josiah with the name of the friend who was coming for them. Then there was a sound of scuffling and I lost the call. We're on our way to the church. Andrew, see if you can raise the chief there."

Andrew spoke rapidly with the Logan City Police Chief, a long time friend of his father's, who promised to send patrol officers to the church.

Tad pulled to a stop behind the cruisers and the three headed for the barrier set up. Flashing their badges, they walked through, looking for any sign of the two. Not seeing either one, their hearts sank.

The chief turned as they approached, shaking his head. "They're not here. One of our officers found Aaron down in his office. He's okay, up on his feet and very angry."

"There's no sign of them? Faith said they were hiding in some trees near here." Andrew turned to look towards the trees back from the church.

"We searched there and found signs of a scuffle as well as this." The chief held out an evidence bag with a broken phone in it. "It looks as if it was deliberately stepped on."

"Do you what the number of the phone is?" Tad spoke up.

"Yes. This is it." The chief handed him a slip of paper with the number.

"It's Josiah's. Let's pray that Faith still has hers."

The chief eyed them. "Care to tell me what's going on and is it related to those arrests you made a bit ago?"

Andrew nodded. "It is. Brownlee was responsible for the murders of Faith Lockwood's parents and her aunt. There's been a group in her hometown that have been demanding protection money and Faith and her uncle have refused to pay. It's come out now that they're after Faith for revenge, not money. Josiah, her husband, got caught in the crossfire and kidnapped. We just got them back together about a week or so ago. They didn't want to go to a safe house, not trusting in the system, and I can't say as I blame them. We have a leak somewhere.

They decided to go out on their own and picked this town, figuring it was large enough they could get lost in. Seems as if it wasn't."

The chief studied the three men in front of him, then excused himself to speak with an officer approaching him. He turned to look at the trees, then turned back to the three waiting for him. He walked back, shaking his head.

"That's quite the tale, Andrew. I know you and I know you don't make up things. I was just told the officers searching found evidence that at least one of them has been hurt. We can't tell which one though."

Andrew drew a deep breath. "That's what we thought had happened. I would suspect it's Josiah, trying to protect Faith. Any sign which way they were taken?"

"It looks as if they took them back through the trees. The men here were likely decoys with others waiting in the trees, thinking that's where they would hide."

"I don't like this, Andrew. We need to find them." Bill turned in a circle, frowning. Then he excused himself, walking towards a woman hovering near the edge of the crime scene.

"Excuse me." The woman looked up at Bill, eyes squinting. "Do you know something about what happened here?"

The woman sighed. "Yeah, I guess I kinda do. A man approached me, asked me to watch for two people, paid me a hundred dollars. I thought I found them, but then I decided just to keep on going, out of town. Only they were watching the bus station and I couldn't get a bus."

"Can you describe him for me?"

"I can do better than that. I found this phone one day, and the camera still works. Here take it. It has his picture on it." The woman thrust the phone into his hand and walked away.

Bill looked down at the phone, then searched for her. How could that be, he wondered? A lost phone shouldn't have enough charge. Something was off here. He turned as he heard footsteps. Andrew stood there.

"What do you have, Bill?"

Bill filled him in on what had transpired. "She says there's a photo on here of the man. Let me see if I can find it."

Andrew's eyes shot to Bill when he saw the picture, then turned to find out where Tad was. "This isn't good, Bill. We've found our leak."

"We have at that. Did you suspect him at all?"

Andrew shook his head, sorrow on his face. "No. I know Tad hasn't either. How deep does this go and how far back?"

"At least as far back as Faith's parents and aunt. Likely even farther." Bill handed Andrew the phone. "You tell him."

"Not on my own. You're the one who talked to her."

Tad turned as he heard Andrew and Bill approaching him, his words halted on his lips at the looks of their faces.

"Andrew? Bill?"

"We found our leak, Tad. It's from your department." Andrew handed him the phone.

Tad froze, his face stilling into new grim lines. "John Graves? Our chief of detectives? That can't be right."

Bill spoke. "That photo was taken by a woman who claims he approached her, paid her to be on the lookout for Faith and Josiah, and call him when she found them. She found them, but never called him. So, how did he know to look here?"

Tad's eyes slid closed. "The call I made to Aaron. He must have heard something. I had made sure no one was around." He spun. "I know I was alone when I made it. That means there has to be some device in my office. What other investigation has been compromised?"

"Brownlee. That's how they knew where and when he'd be where he was."

Tad pulled out his own phone and made a call. "I can't reach him. He's on duty too. Let me see who I can get to find him."

Andrew turned as he heard his name called. "Angus. Heard you were headed this way."

"What's going on, Andrew? Faith called me to come get her and I find this?"

Andrew studied the younger man in front of him, wondering how he fit into the picture. "I guess you've heard what's been going on?"

Angus nodded. "I've had letters too. Faith talked to me about hers. Is this what it's all about?"

Andrew made a quick decision. "It is. It seems that the group have wanted Faith to enact some kind of revenge. They nabbed her and Josiah today before anyone could get here."

Angus paled. "No! Not that! They're a vicious group."

Andrew nodded. "That they are. Anything you care to tell me?"

Angus shook his head. "I've been faced with the same as Faith has. I put in reports but I hear the officer I put them in to has been relieved of his duties."

"Brownlee?" At the nod, Andrew sighed. "And now he's nowhere to be found."

"What can I do, Andrew?"

"Pray and pray hard, Angus. Hang around for a while. I want to talk to you further once I can get more information."

osiah rolled over to his side, fighting the nausea and dizziness that accompanied his movements. His eyes flickered open and closed. He was unable to keep them open. He heard movement around him before the darkness closed back in.

Faith sat beside Josiah, her hand on his hand, willing him to wake up again. They had hit him too hard, she thought, those men who had taken them captive. How did that happen, she wondered? We didn't see anyone behind us when we went through the trees. Her head sank down and she blinked, trying to stay awake. Unable able to, she stretched out beside Josiah, one hand on his arm.

The man in charge opened the door and stepped through, his steps heavy on the old wooden floor. He stood, narrowed eyes staring down at the two. He wanted them awake. His men had gone too far, he thought, in how they had treated Josiah. He needed him alive to get Faith to do what he wanted. His eyes raised, he stared out the bare dirt-clad window into the night sky. He had had them taken from town to an old house he owned just outside the city boundary. This was where he planned to question Faith, and this was where their bodies would be buried when he was done.

He turned and walked away, the floor boards bouncing under his heavy steps. Time had not been kind to him, or rather, his fat-filled diet had not been kind to him. His weight made it difficult for him to move most days and some days made it difficult for him to breath. He had been told his time was short and he wanted to exact his revenge before his life ended.

Hours later, Josiah stirred again, his hand coming to his head, finding the spot that was sore. Not again, Lord, he thought. Why me? He rolled to his back, his eyes opening and closing and finally staying open. He looked around at the dirty empty room, noting the peeling wallpaper, chipping paint and water stains on the ceiling and around the window. Hearing a faint sound, he sat up, waiting until his head stopped spinning, and then looked around.

"Faith! Wake up, Faith!" He reached to touch her shoulder.

Faith jerked away, her hand flying up to protect herself. She struggled when it was caught, until she heard her name in a familiar voice.

"Josiah? Where are we? How's your head?"

"My head's fine. Are you okay?" Josiah reached to wrap his wife in his arms. "I have no idea where we are. Those men hit hard."

"I know. They knocked you out and then stuffed us into that vehicle. I couldn't see anything." She chewed her bottom lip and then rose, walking over to the window. She drew in her breath as the floor shook underneath her. "This must be a really old, worn down building. The floor doesn't feel safe."

Josiah rose as well, walking carefully towards her. "What floor are we on?"

"The first floor by the looks of it." She felt around the window. "It's too swollen to open and I don't know if there is anyone around to hear if we broke the window."

Josiah leaned forward, touching his head to the window. "It's not that big a drop, but we need to be sure we're alone before we do anything."

They turned as they heard the key being turned in the lock, Josiah tucking Faith behind him.

"Well, well, well. You're up and on your feet, are you?"

The oily voice grated across Faith's ears. She peeked around Josiah and drew in her breath. She knew him, quite well in fact.

"Walter Broadbent! Now why doesn't that surprise me?"

"So you do know me after all, Faith. It's a shame you had to refuse to pay your money. That would have avoided all this."

Faith snorted. "Not likely. You're after revenge, not money. You've been afraid all these years that it would come out that you've been responsible for murders. How many, Walter? Just how many?"

"You'll never live to tell anyone, my dear. I'll tell you. At least twelve but no

one ever caught on. Until that man there."
His finger pointed at Josiah. "I heard he was
digging around. That's why the ante was
upped for you. You both will never leave
this place alive." With that, he turned and
walked away.

Josiah turned back to Faith, drawing
her into his arms. "We'll get out, Faith. I
promise you that. I don't have my phone.
Do you still have yours?"

She nodded, withdrawing it from her
pocket. "They didn't search me, thankfully.
Here."

"Keep a listen out for someone
coming back, okay?" Joseph thought about
his message, knowing it would have to be
succinct. He send a quick message to both
Bill and Andrew, praying that they got it and
could follow the signal to find them.

"Did you get through?" Faith's quiet
whisper barely reached him.

He walked towards her.   "I did.
Hopefully they'll be here soon."

"I don't think we're far from Oak City.
They didn't drive for that long."

"In the county?"

She nodded. "I think so. I really wasn't paying that much attention, I was so worried about you."

He reached to touch his head, grimacing as he found the sore point. "I'm okay. They didn't hurt you?"

She shook her head. "Not yet, but I'm sure that's what's planned."

Josiah drew her away from the door and to the floor across from it so they could lean on the wall. "Tell me about this man."

"He was mayor at the time my parents were murdered. He didn't get elected back in after that one term, and he's always blamed someone for that. His wife left him soon after and took their children. The last I heard, they had moved across the country and had no contact with him. There have always been rumours about him, that he was involved in criminal activities." She shuddered, knowing that if Andrew and Tad didn't reach them in time, they would be just another couple of murders Walter would be accountable for.

"What does he actually do?"

"He has a scrap yard in the county and a metal recycling shop in the town. We've often wondered how he could live like he does on what he makes from them. He had no rich relative to leave him money."

"Sounds like a nasty person. Why would he kill your parents?"

"From what Uncle Seth has said, there was a protection racket going on when Dad was alive. Dad refused to pay, found out who the lower men in the organization were and turned them in. No one would talk and say how the leader was, but they always suspected Walter. I guess they were right."

Andrew ran for his car, Bill and Tad in tow, and flew from the church parking lot, heading for the house where they now knew Josiah and Faith were being held. Lord, let us be in time. They had kept up the command centre at the church, and the three had stopped there that morning for news.

"Who owns that house?" Andrew shot the question at Tad.

Tad was reading his emails, scrolling through to find the one he wanted. "Here it is. Samuel, Josiah's friend, came through. It's registered to a Walter Broadbent."

"Broadbent!" Tad turned to stare at Bill sitting in the back seat. "He's big in the recycling and metal business. Didn't he used to be mayor?"

Andrew nodded. "He did. From what Seth has said, he's suspected all along that Walter had something to do with the murders of Faith's parents and Noah's mother. Pray we reach them in time, men. Because if we don't, he'll be long gone and we'll only have two more bodies to bury and families to inform of murders."

Bill paled at the thought. "How do we do this, Andrew?"

"I have had April working on warrants for us. See if she has them ready for us. We knew he had this property, but it's so rundown that we never figured he'd use it for anything. He's been behind in the taxes on it and the county's taking it over next week."

"But if he destroys it now, he'll get any insurance on it."

Andrew's face filled with more stern and somber lines. Bill's hands froze on his phone at the thought.

"So, unless we can get in and get them, they'll be buried in the building, won't they? He'll find some what of knocking it down?" Bill's eyes searched ahead of him. "There's the road, Andrew. We'll need to go in on foot." He turned as he heard vehicles stopping behind them. "April's here and she's waving paperwork at us."

"Good girl." Andrew walked towards her, their conversation quiet. He then turned to Tad. "This is now in our county, so I'll have to take the lead on this."

"Not a problem, Andrew. Just let me know where you want me."

"Right beside me, you and Bill both. Okay, this is what we're facing people. Listen up."

Chapter 23

*W*alter stood, watching the two standing in front of him, a sneer on his face.

"You really think we didn't know you had a phone on you? It won't work, my girl. You'll be dead before they even get here." He raised a weapon, pointing it at them as he stepped into the room.

An ominous crack and creak sounded as he stepped onto a softer part of the floor. The floor gave way beneath him, his weapon discharging at the ceiling as he fell through. Josiah pulled Faith back towards him as the ceiling creaked. The water and rain had done their work, weakening the structure overhead. A crack and the ceiling caved, taking down the rest of the floor and the side wall.

Josiah heard Faith scream as they fell, his arms wrapped tight around her. Debris hit them, and they both lay still, buried under the debris.

Andrew stopped as he heard the sound of the collapsing building. Then he was running for the building, sliding to a halt as he saw the partially collapsed structure. Bill was on the phone calling for help even as they continued to run towards it. Officers spread out, searching for Walter's henchmen, arresting them as they were uncovered from their hiding places.

Their faces white, Tad and Andrew stared at each other, then back at the building.

"Could they have survived?" Tad ran for the back of the building where the most damage was.

"I have no idea. It doesn't look stable enough for us to search it, either." Andrew stared at the building. "I pray they are still alive. If they're not, I can only hope they didn't suffer."

Tad nodded and turned as he heard the sirens and sounds of the vehicles approaching.

With emergency lighting in place, the firemen worked through the night to stabilize what they could of the structure to make is safe enough for them to enter. Finally in the early morning, the fire chief deemed it safe enough for his men to go in. Cautiously moving aside debris, two of them dropped down into the basement, and searched, the beams from their search lights hitting the darkness. Pointing, they crawled carefully to the point one thought they had seen clothing. Moving aside the smaller bits of debris, they stopped, then frantically reached for feel for a pulse.

One stayed as the other crawled rapidly back, calling for help and backboards. Two more men dropped down, the backboards following them.

Tad and Andrew watched, moving as close as they could. Someone had been found, but who and was that person still alive? Tension was mounting as they looked to the sky, knowing that a storm was moving in. Please Lord, Andrew prayed, please let it be them and let them be alive. You've promised protection against evil and a shelter in times of trouble. Let that have happened for these two. He turned as he heard soft footsteps approaching. Bill was back.

"You've got Seth and Silas?"

Bill nodded. "I have. They're tucked away in the chief's office for now, to keep them away from the press. The press are hungry and vocal."

"I imagine they would be," Tad responded.

"What do we have going on here?" Bill strained to see.

"They've found someone, but I haven't heard who yet." Andrew turned as the fire chief approached.

"Andrew. It's been a long night, but we have your two friends. They're working on getting them out now."

"They're alive?"

The chief nodded. "They are. We can't assess them properly down there but as soon as they're out, we'll be heading for the Emergency. We could use an escort."

"You'll have it, Chief. My men and the men from your town are anxious to be of help." He turned as the first backboard was raised from the basement and carried to a stretcher. He could see the paramedics working rapidly, then wheeling the stretcher to a waiting ambulance.

"Go, Bill. Go with whoever that is."

The chief spoke. "It's the male, Josiah is it?"

Andrew nodded. "That's his name."

"He was protecting her, you know. She was under his body, so it looked at first as if we only had one person."

Andrew nodded, waiting anxiously for Faith to be brought up. When she was, he headed for the stretcher. This time, he would ride with her. Tad followed.

"Where do you want me, Andrew?"

"How about in the lead escort vehicle? Take mine."

"I'm on it. I'll have an officer bring their family over to the hospital for you."

"Thanks." Andrew stood, heart in his mouth as he watched them work on Faith. Please, Lord, let her be all right.

"We're ready to transport, sir. Are you with us?"

Andrew nodded and slipped into the back of the ambulance, taking his seat, his eyes on Faith.

"How is she?"

"She's alive. That was her husband with her?" At Andrew's nod, the paramedic continued, "He protected her from the debris and as much of the fall as he could, I think. We'll know more once she's been assessed."

Seth and Silas almost ran through the door when Bill let them out before going to park his cruiser. They searched frantically for Andrew, finally finding him standing among officers. He saw them, excused himself and came towards them.

"Andrew?" Seth's voice was broken and unsteady. "Tell me they're alive?"

Andrew nodded. "They are. Did anyone explain to you where we found them?" At their nod, he continued, "Josiah took the brunt of the fall and the debris coming down on him from what the firemen said. The physicians are assessing them now. They're aware you two were on your way in. I've had word they'll be coming out shortly."

"Tell me you caught the man who was behind this." The agony in Silas' voice tore at Andrew and Tad as he walked up to them.

"I just got word that the firemen found his body. They're waiting for heavy equipment to come in and move some of the heavier debris before they bring him out."

Seth turned his eyes to Andrew and read the knowledge there. "Who was it, Andrew? I know you have the name."

"It was Walter Broadbent."

"Broadbent?" Seth's voice rose as he said the name. Then he nodded. "That makes sense. He always had more money to flash around than came in from his businesses. No one liked him when he was mayor. He's the one responsible for the murders?"

Andrew nodded. "We're working through his home and businesses now, but we've found documentation and evidence that implicate him as the brains behind the protection racket and also behind the murders. We've found evidence of multiple murders that he's covered up well. He's gone on to face a harsher Judge than he would have faced here."

"That he has." Silas turned to face the exam rooms. "Any word on how long it will take to get word?"

Andrew shook his head. "They didn't say. There's coffee over there, I'm not sure how good it will be. Go grab some, then find a chair."

Hours later Andrew stood by Josiah's bedside, watching as he glared at the nurse. He smiled. Yes, Josiah was fine. A broken arm, bumps, bruises. God had protected him.

"So, fill me in, Andrew. I know you've already talked to Faith."

"I have. Both of you were protected greatly in that fall. The debris made a canopy over you. Do you feel that God was there?" At Josiah's nod, he continued to speak. "They've found Walter's body. He was the one behind it all, including the younger Brownlee and his destruction of evidence. It was what we expected with Faith. Revenge. That's what started up the whole protection thing again. They couldn't go after her for protection money without it seeming strange. His mind was starting to twist and lose focus on what he had now, concentrating of perceived slights and losses. He was responsible for the murders of Faith's people as well as a number of others.

"Bill tracked down that object you found on the walkway. It was a miniature souvenir motorcycle wheel he had been given and that protection fellow had lifted from his desk. He didn't know it was missing, apparently.

"We found out that it was young Brownlee who hit you that night. Whoever it was removed him before he could hurt you more."

"I know Seth gave Bill a note. Did he say what was in it?"

"Apparently, Seth remembered some of the names from the first protection racket and gave it to Bill to run down the people. He was still working through that when Broadbent kidnapped you two. And I understand that you came up with a few names and dollar amounts yourself and passed it on to Broadbent."

"I did. Guess I shouldn't have, but I wanted to flush him out and get this over with."

"It all helped, Josiah, it all helped in the end." He turned as he heard a sound at the door. "I understand you're being moved upstairs to a room. Faith will be in the same room. We still want you under guard until we ensure we have everyone involved arrested." He paused. "We found out who shot Watson. It was the father of one of the young nurses he took advantage of and who committed suicide."

Epilogue

*F*aith Silverthorn turned from the work room in the new building. Both Beth and Will were there, Will not just working on their books. Even in a wheelchair, Will was able to help with the soldering. Stringbean had managed to build a table at the right height for him. Her stained glass business was flourishing. In the six months since their adventure, she had been able to expand to teaching classes and found she really enjoyed that. Her work had taken on more of a theme for Scripture-based designs than it had. Zeke's church wanted her to do some windows for them, but she declined, passing them on to a good friend of hers instead who specialized in that.   Seth continued to help in the work room, but had almost full-time work packaging and shipping the orders. They would have to hire soon, she thought.

She stopped in the doorway of the office, watching as Josiah worked away on a website design. He had transitioned his work as well to designing for Christian organizations and artists and was enjoying the change. He turned as he heard her behind him and reached out a hand.

She slipped down onto his lap and hugged him, his arms around her. They were safe now, but the remnants of what they had gone through still crept to the surface ever once in a while.

"How was your day, Sweetheart?" Josiah dropped a kiss on the mouth he loved to touch. "Get your new designs done?"

"I have. I'm thinking I need to hire and train at least one or two more in the work room. Our orders are getting ahead of us again. God has certainly given us more than what we ever asked for, business wise."

Josiah nodded. "That he has. For both of us. He also took the broken glass we were both made of and created something brand new and beautiful." He stopped, his eyes tracing the face he loved. "But that's not what's bothering you, is it?"

She shook her head, then laid it against his shoulder. "No, it's not. Sometimes I wonder why we had to go through what we did. I know God was there, but I still need to know from a human point of view."

"I don't think we ever will know the full reason here on earth, Faith. God used you to help others and stop evil."

"I know. Noah says the same thing." She looked over at her desk and sighed. "I need to do some more designing, but I'm just not in the mood today." She looked at her husband, stood, and grasped his hand. "Come on, let's walk over and see how Stringbean and his crew are making out on our house. There's one room I'm anxious to see."

Josiah's eyebrow rose. "There is. And which one would that be?"

She turned, a sparkle of mischief in her eyes and she grinned at him. "The nursery for our future children." She ran as he dropped her hand in surprise.

Shocked Josiah stood there. Then with a shout of laughter, he ran after her. "Faith, what aren't you telling me?"

"I just did, sweetheart. I'm off to the nursery to see how it will work for our "future" children."

Josiah caught up with her and spun her around, then dropped a kiss on her upturned face. "Not so distant, are they?" When she shook her head, he hugged her. "God has been good to us. Your example led me back to Him. And now we'll raise our children to love and honour him."

Arm in arm they headed for the house they were building, dreams already running through their minds and conversation.

Dear Friends

Thank you so much for picking up *Broken Glass*, the first in a new series entitled *His Warriors*. The premise of this series is based on the spiritual warfare and armour we need to put on every day as we fight a war. We don't fight the war that Josiah and Faith did, at least I hope we don't. But we each have a battle we're involved in, whatever it may be. Know that the battle and war are already won. God has given the victory, even though there are days it feels like we're losing. I have had many of those days myself, and I have to remind myself that God cares for and loves me so much. He has me in the hollow of His hand each and every day. Another reminder I like to give myself is the prayer in the Garden. Do you know that Christ prayed for you even back then? He knew who you were all those years ago.

Anyone pick up on the play on characters in the book? No? Old Wiley and Roadie. No? Still don't get it. All right, I'll explain. When I was growing up back in the 1960s (yep, I'm dating myself, aren't I?), my Dad worked long hours. We could count on him being home on Saturday nights for sure. One of my treasured memories is the smell of homemade fries and hamburgers that my Mom would be making as my Dad, my older sister, and I would be seated in the living room, watching The Bugs Bunny and Roadrunner show. (Got it yet?) My favourite character was Wile E. Coyote, who tried so hard but just couldn't get Roadrunner. There, you got it, didn't you? I sometimes feel like the coyote, trying hard and not getting anywhere. Then I remind myself, I'm right where God wants me, in my community, in my church, and in the medical office I work in. Until He says it's time to move on, I stay.

Or how about Georgia and her huge curiosity? My nieces and nephew had a cartoon they lived to watch, named Curious George, a monkey who was always getting himself into predicaments because of his curiosity. I tell my little tuxedo cat I should have named her Georgia or Georgette because of her curiosity.

God bless each one of you as you walk with Him through each and every day. Remember, He knows your name, has since before time began. He has given us the victory in any battle that we fight, provided

us with the armour and strength we need.
We are not and never will be alone.

Ronna

* 9 7 8 1 9 8 9 0 0 0 3 0 4 *